PRANKENSTEIN

Prankenstein

THE BOOK OF
CRAZY MISCHIEF

EDITED BY

Ruskin Bond
Jerry Pinto

talking
CUB

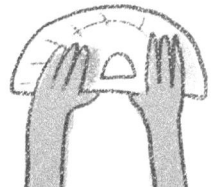

TALKING CUB
Published by Speaking Tiger Publishing Pvt. Ltd
4381/4, Ansari Road, Daryaganj
New Delhi 110002

Published in Talking Cub by Speaking Tiger in 2017
Edition copyright © Speaking Tiger 2017
Illustrations copyright © Lavanya Naidu 2017

Copyright for the individual pieces vests with the respective authors
'The Helping Hand' by R.K. Narayan published with permission
from the legal heirs of R.K. Narayan

ISBN: 978-93-87164-44-4
eISBN: 978-93-87164-26-0

10 9 8 7 6 5 4 3 2 1

Typeset in Cardo by Jojy Philip
Printed at Sanat Printers, Kundli

CONTENTS

MISCHIEF
IN
SCHOOL

THE THINGS THEY SHOULDN'T ASK YOU

Jerry Pinto

PARENTS ask the oddest questions.

What if you told the truth, all the time? They say that they'd like that.

Yeah sure, they'd like that.

See what would happen. I don't know about you, but my parents would throw me out of the house if I told them the truth.

'What do you do with your school books?'
Well, first there's book cricket. In order to get a high score, every fool knows you have to bend the spine at pages 4, 6, 14, 16, 24, 26, 34, 36 etc. That way, each time you open your book, you get a four or a six. Otherwise, if you hit 10, 20, or something like that, you get out.

Then there's the open window that I sit next to, see? Yesterday, a fly came in so I whacked it with my atlas. That left a yucky mark so I tried to rub it off with my hankie and some water. The cover got spoilt so I pulled it off. I wanted to tell you to cover it again but you were busy so I forgot and it got dog-eared.

And yes, yes, there's the underlining. Mrs Furtardo makes us underline the important stuff. Then she decides that it's not important so you have to rub it out again. I collect all the rubbings because Shakil says you can melt them down and get a new rubber. But I didn't know where to collect them so I tore a piece of the last page—it's an empty page, Ma—and I wrapped the rubbings in that.

And when I came back from physical training period, I was sweating, so I put the book under my arm so I wouldn't wet my mathematics fair book. It still got wet.

And I study from them.

'What do you do with your handkerchiefs?'
Shakil says he knows how to make invisible ink.

He doesn't.

That's what happened.

'What do you do with your socks?'
You don't like scorpions, do you Ma? I don't like them either. So when Rajesh found a scorpion in the graveyard, he put it under a coconut shell and he called me. He only thinks of me when things like this happen. So I went there and I took a stone and I put it in my sock. Then I kicked aside the shell like Messi and I hit the scorpion with the sock. *Thappachchch.*

Scorpion masala.

But don't throw it away, Ma. That's a very useful sock. I can take it for fishing on the beach in the rock pools. No, *because* it has a hole I can use it. See, what you do, you take some of your tiffin, something with a nice smell and you rub it along the hole. Then you lower the sock into the rock pool where the baby fish swim. They all come *dhapaadhap*. Then when they swim into the hole, you turn the sock slowly and lift them out in the part that doesn't have a hole. We play scores: one fish, one point.

'What do you do with your compass box?'

I do geometry stuff and things and all but when my back is scratchy then I use the ruler to get at the bits I can't scratch. Why don't we have longer arms, Ma? Why don't we have foldy arms that make it easy for us to scratch our backs? Of course, I wash my back. I wash it very well, thank you, but maybe the bits I don't reach are the bits I scratch.

And my divider got blunt because we were playing Arjun-Arjun. Shakil uses his to draw six-petalled flowers on the desk, you know that one where the last arc completes the last two petals and if it's perfect then it meets on the edge of the circle. But that's kid's stuff, who's going to draw like that? Or even draw a gravestone and write inside it, 'This is in memory of all those who died of boredom'. Besides, you get blamed and they give you solid dose for all that. But if you straighten your divider and make it a straight line, then it becomes a dart, and if you draw a dartboard on the blackboard, you can play Arjun-Arjun. Fun comes.

The protractor is for Krishna-Krishna. If you put it on your finger and you whirl, it becomes a sudarshan chakra. That Alan has a foreign protractor which is a full round thing, so he thinks he can be Krishna all the time. But you also have to throw your chakra while running and make sure it hits one of the Kauravas. Alan can never do that; he never even tries. He doesn't want to throw his protractor because it might break.

'What do you do with your pens?'
I don't know. I know you gave me a new pen on my birthday and I know that you said that it was the last pen you were ever going to give me and that I would have to write with my fingers for the rest of my life. (Gosh, how fat my handwriting would become and how many books I would use up.) I know you tied it up on a string and you put it round my neck, but when I was running to school, it bounced up and hit me on the mouth. So I put it in my pocket and when I went to school, it wasn't there. I thought there was a hole in my pocket but there isn't. And I came back and asked everyone whether they had seen a pen fall from my pocket but no one had seen one or they must have taken it for themselves, robbers.

So I don't know. I really don't know. But I have a test tomorrow and Mrs Ahuja will not let me start if I don't have my pen so please...

'Why don't you eat your tiffin?'
Oh that.

I ate the chocolate biscuit yesterday but I ate it on the way to school because it doesn't look nice to eat a chocolate biscuit without sharing it. And I didn't want to share it.

Otherwise?

I don't eat my tiffin because I'm not hungry. See, if I eat it at recess, I get full and then I can't run so I always think I'll eat the good stuff and then play but if you don't get to the compound early enough, the game has already started so there's no fun. And once you start a game, you can't stop if you're winning because no one will let you stop and you have to give the losers a chance to win. And you can't stop if you're losing because only bad sports stop when they're losing. And then return matches have to be fixed and sometimes there's homework; so where's the time. And if I eat it at lunch break then I'm not hungry, and you complain that I don't eat my lunch.

And anyway, I don't like what you put in my box.

'What did you learn in school today?'
There's this wild plant in the graveyard, very nice. It has these white flowers and funny seeds like maces and if you eat any part of it, you go mad. Really. I asked Mr Kazi and he said, 'Yes, datura is like that.' Datura. That's the name. I was thinking, so much fun to put datura in everyone's tea in the staffroom, then they would all go mad and say they were Napoleon or King George the Something.

And Celestine's father gets so drunk that he falls into his lunch. That makes me feel bad for Celestine who is a good guy and knows lots of stuff, so what if he is a repeater? But I don't know because Celestine told me about it and he was laughing. I felt funny but I smiled also and then I didn't like that I smiled. But what to do with your face when someone says something like that?

When you sneeze, your whole body stops. Everything.

Even your digestion. So you can't sneeze with your eyes open or you would be seeing and then your body would be doing something so you wouldn't be able to sneeze. So if you meet a spy who is pretending to sneeze, it's easy to tell he's faking. Because he would keep his eyes open since he would want to spy all the time so he would pretend that he was sneezing and keep his eyes open. If he was pretending.

And if you carry your bag on your head, you don't grow. If you go to a gym too early, you don't grow. If you jump over someone's head, they don't grow.

'No, what did you learn in class?'
I'm telling you what I learnt in class. Oh studies? Nothing.

'How come you can get up at any time on a holiday but you're always late for school?'
That one's so easy, you should know. I don't like school. I like holidays. So I can get up at any time on a holiday because I want lots of holiday time. I can't get up on a school day because I know it's a school day and I know that as soon as I get up, I have to rush to the bathroom and have a bath and pack my bag and start worrying about school.

And there's always something to worry about in school. School is about worrying only. They make it like that. They want you to worry. Mrs Ahuja says, 'Everyone fails in the sixth standard.' Mrs D'Mello says, 'Sit up straight, clear your desks, clear your minds and pay attention.' That means it is tough. And some of the teachers don't like you. Just like that. And when they don't like you, there's nothing you can do and nothing you can say. Last year, my class teacher, Mr Patil, didn't like me. First day only he said, 'You are a trouble-maker, come up and sit under my nose.' And then the whole year, he would check me first. 'Say the poem. Show me your homework. Have you brought your compass box?' But he was better than Mrs D'Souza. When she takes up poetry this year, she says, 'Say the first and third verse.' And if you stop to say the second verse in your head, she minuses one mark. And then there's mental maths surprise test and there's art class in which you have to have your brushes and your paints and your compass box and your drawing book and it has to be covered with nice paper. The paper you put? I thought it was pretty but the art teacher said, 'I told you to put pretty paper. Tell your mother next time.' So I couldn't tell her that my mother put it on so I just hate her. Then she says, 'Memory drawing. Draw a bullock-cart race.' I told her I haven't seen a bullock-cart race, how I'll have a memory of it and she gives me a note in my class diary saying I am rude and you think I have been rude and I can't even tell you that I wasn't rude or that I hate her because she thinks you don't know what pretty paper is. Then, 'Have you brought your composition book? Yes, today is grammar period but I said quite clearly bring your composition books.' And, 'Have you done your environmental studies project?' And 'Conjugate aller in the recent past.' And. 'What is x plus y the whole cubed minus x minus y the whole cubed?'

No one asks you what you want to do. No one asks you what you think. No one even wants to know. So why should I want to go to school?

'*So do you want to drop out of school and be illiterate and make chapatis for your friends' tiffin boxes?*'

As though I can answer that.

'*Do you?*'

Yes. Because I hate school.

No. Because I am on the football team and they won't let me play if I'm not in school.

THE HELPING HAND

R.K. Narayan

LYING in bed, Swaminathan realized with a shudder that it was Monday morning. It looked as though only a moment ago it had been the last period on Friday but Monday was already here. He hoped that a earthquake would reduce the school building to dust but that good building—Albert Mission School—had withstood similar prayers for over a hundred years now. At nine o'clock Swaminathan wailed, 'I have a headache.' His mother said, 'Why don't you go to school in a *jutka*?

'So that I may be completely dead at the other end? Have you any idea what it means to be jolted in a *jutka*?'

'Have you many important lessons today?'

'Important! Bah! That geography teacher has been teaching the same lesson for over a year now. And we have arithmetic, which means for a whole period we are going to be beaten by the teacher ... Important lessons!'

And Mother generously suggested that Swaminathan might stay at home.

At nine-thirty, when he ought to have been shouting in the school prayer hall, Swaminathan was lying on the bench in Mother's room. Father asked him, 'Have you no school today?'

'Headache,' Swaminathan replied.

'Nonsense. Dress up and go.'

'Headache.'

'Loaf about less on Sundays and you will be without a headache on Monday.'

Swaminathan knew how stubborn his father could be and changed his tactics. 'I can't go so late to the class.'

'I agree, but you'll have to; it is your own fault. You should have asked me before deciding to stay away.'

'What will the teacher think if I go so late?'

'Tell him you had a headache and so are late.'

'He will beat me if I say so.'

'Will he? Let us see. What is his name?'

'Samuel.'

'Does he beat the boys?'

'He is very violent, especially with boys who come late. Some days ago a boy was made to stay on his knees for a whole period in a corner of the class because he came late, and that after getting six cuts from the cane and having his ears twisted. I wouldn't like to go late to Samuel's class.'

'If he is so violent, why not tell your Headmaster about it?'

'They say that even the Headmaster is afraid of him. He is such a violent man.'

And then Swaminathan gave a lurid account of Samuel's

violence; how when he started caning he would not stop till he saw blood on the boy's hand which he made the boy press to his forehead like a vermilion marking. Swami hoped that with this his father would be made to see that he couldn't go to his class late. But Father's behaviour took an unexpected turn. He became excited. 'What do these swines mean by beating our children? They must be driven out of service. I will see ...'

The result was that he proposed to send Swaminathan late to his class as a kind of challenge. He was also going to send a letter with Swaminathan for the Headmaster. No amount of protest from Swaminathan was of any avail: he had to go to school.

By the time he was ready Father had composed a long letter to the Headmaster, put it in an envelope and sealed it.

'What have you written, Father?' Swaminathan asked apprehensively.

'Nothing for you. Give it to your Headmaster and go to your class.'

'Have you written anything about our teacher Samuel?'

'Plenty of things about him. When your Headmaster reads it he will probably dismiss Samuel from the school and hand him over to the police.'

'What has he done, Father?'

'Well, there is a full account of everything he has done, in this letter. Give it to your Headmaster and go to your class. You must bring an acknowledgement from him in the evening.'

Swaminathan went to school feeling that he was the worst perjurer on earth. His conscience bothered him, he wasn't at all sure if he had been accurate in his description of Samuel. He could not decide how much of what he had said was imagined and how much of it was real. He stopped for a moment on the roadside to make up his mind about Samuel: he was not such a bad man after all. Personally he was much more genial than the rest; often he cracked a joke or two centring around Swaminathan's inactions, and Swaminathan took it as a mark of Samuel's personal regard for him. But there was no doubt that he treated people badly …

His cane skinned people's hands. Swaminathan cast his mind about for an instance of this. There was none within his knowledge. Years and years ago he was reputed to have skinned the knuckles of a boy in the First Standard and made him smear the blood on his face. No one had actually seen it. But year after year the story persisted among the boys … Swaminathan's head was dizzy with confusion in regard to Samuel's character—whether he was good or bad, whether he deserved the allegations in the letter or not … he felt an impulse to run home and beg his father to take back the letter. But Father was an obstinate man.

As he approached the yellow building he realized that he was perjuring himself and was ruining his teacher. Probably the Headmaster would dismiss Samuel and then the police would chain him and put him in jail. For all this disgrace, humiliation and suffering who would be responsible? Swaminathan shuddered. The more he thought of Samuel, the more he grieved for him—the dark face, his small red-streaked eyes, his thin line of moustache, his unshaven cheek and chin, his yellow coat; everything filled Swaminathan with sorrow. As he felt the bulge of the letter in his pocket he felt like an executioner.

For a moment he was angry with his father and wondered why he should not fling into the gutter the letter of a man so unreasonable and stubborn.

As he entered the school gate an idea occurred to him, a sort of solution. He wouldn't deliver the letter to the Headmaster immediately, but at the end of the day—to that extent he would disobey his father and exercise his independence. There was nothing wrong in it, and Father would not know it anyway. If the letter was given at the end of the day there was a chance that Samuel might do something to justify the latter.

Swaminathan stood at the entrance to his class. Samuel was teaching arithmetic. He looked at Swaminathan for a moment. Swaminathan stood hoping that Samuel would fall on him and tear his skin off. But Samuel merely asked, 'Are you just coming to the class?'

'Yes, sir.'

'You are half an hour late.'

'I know it.' Swaminathan hoped that he would be attacked now. He almost prayed: 'God of Thirupathi, please make Samuel beat me.'

'Why are you late?'

Swaminathan wanted to reply, 'Just to see what you can do.' But he merely said, 'I have a headache, sir.'

'Then why did you come to the school at all?'

A most unexpected question from Samuel. 'My father said that I shouldn't miss the class, sir,' said Swaminathan.

This seemed to impress Samuel. 'Your father is quite right; a very sensible man. We want more parents like him.'

'Oh, you poor worm!' Swaminathan thought. 'You don't

know what my father has done to you.' He was more puzzled than ever about Samuel's character.

'All right, go to your seat. Have you still a headache?'

'Slightly, sir.'

Swaminathan went to his seat with a bleeding heart. He had never met a man so good as Samuel. The teacher was inspecting the home lessons, which usually produced (at least, according to Swaminathan's impression) scenes of great violence. Notebooks would be flung at faces, boys would be abused, caned and made to stand up on benches. But today Samuel appeared to have developed more tolerance and gentleness. He pushed away the bad books, just touched people with the cane, never made anyone stand up for more than a few minutes. Swaminathan's turn came. He almost thanked God for the chance.

'Swaminathan, where is your homework?'

'I have not done any homework, sir,' he said blandly.

There was a pause.

'Why—headache?' asked Samuel.

'Yes, sir.'

'All right, sit down.' Swaminathan sat down, wondering what had come over Samuel. The period came to an end, and he felt desolate. The last period for the day was again taken by Samuel. He came this time to teach them Indian history. The period began at three-forty-five and ended at four-thirty. Swaminathan had sat through the previous periods thinking acutely. He could not devise any means of provoking Samuel. When the clock struck four he felt desperate. Half an hour more. Samuel was reading the red text, the portion describing Vasco da Gama's arrival in India. The boys listened in half-languor.

Swaminathan suddenly asked at the top of his voice, 'Why did not Columbus come to India, sir?'

'He lost his way.'

'I can't believe it; it is unbelievable, sir.'

'Why?'

'Such a great man. Would he have not known the way?'

'Don't shout. I can hear you quite well.'

'I am not shouting, sir; this is my ordinary voice which God has given me. How can I help it?'

'Shut up and sit down.'

Swaminathan sat down, feeling slightly happy at his success. The teacher threw a puzzled, suspicious glance at him and resumed his lessons.

His next chance occurred when Sankar of the first bench got up and asked, 'Sir, was Vasco da Gama the very first person to come to India?'

Before the teacher could answer, Swaminathan shouted from the back bench, 'That's what they say.'

The teacher and all the boys looked at him. The teacher was puzzled by Swaminathan's obtrusive behaviour today. 'Swaminathan, you are shouting again.'

'I am not shouting, sir. How can I help my voice, given by God?' The school clock struck a quarter-hour. A quarter more. Swaminathan felt that he had to do something drastic in fifteen minutes. Samuel had no doubt scowled at him and snubbed him, but it was hardly adequate. Swaminathan felt that with a little more effort Samuel could be made to deserve dismissal and imprisonment.

The teacher came to the end of a section in the text-book

and stopped. He proposed to spend the remaining few minutes putting questions to the boys. He ordered the whole class to put away their books, and asked someone in the second row, 'What is the date of Vasco da Gama's arrival in India?'

Swaminathan shot up and screeched, '1648 December 20.'

'You needn't shout,' said the teacher. He asked, 'Has your headache made you mad?'

'I have no headache now, sir,' replied the thunderer brightly.

'Sit down, you idiot.' Swaminathan felt thrilled at being called an idiot. 'If you get up again I will cane you,' said the teacher. Swaminathan sat down, feeling happy at the promise. The teacher then asked, 'I am going to put a few questions on the Mughal period. Among the Mughal emperors, whom would you call the greatest, whom the strongest and whom the most religious emperor?'

Swaminathan got up. As soon as he was seen, the teacher said emphatically, 'Sit down.'

'I want to answer, sir.'

'Sit down.'

'No, sir; I want to answer.'

'What did I say I'd do if you got up again?'

'You said you would cane me and peel the skin off my knuckles and make me press it on my forehead.'

'All right; come here.'

Swaminathan left his seat joyfully and hopped onto the platform. The teacher took out his cane from the drawer and shouted angrily, 'Open your hand, you little devil.' He whacked three wholesome cuts off each palm. Swaminathan received them without blanching. After half a dozen the teacher asked, 'Will these do, or do you want some more?'

Swaminathan merely held out his hand again, and received two more; and the bell rang. Swaminathan jumped down from the platform with a light heart though his hands were smarting. He picked up his books, took out the letter lying in his pocket and ran to the Headmaster's room. He found the door locked.

He asked the peon, 'Where is the Headmaster?'

'Why do you want him?'

'My father has sent a letter for him.'

'He has taken the afternoon off and won't come back for a week. You can give the letter to the Assistant Headmaster. He will be here now.'

'Who is he?'

'Your teacher, Samuel. He will be here in a second.'

Swaminathan fled from the place. As soon as he reached home with the letter, Father remarked, I knew you wouldn't deliver it, you coward.'

'I swear our Headmaster is on leave,' Swaminathan began.

Father replied, 'Don't lie in addition to being a coward...'

Swami held up the envelope and said, 'I will give this to the Headmaster as soon as he is back...' Father snatched it from his hand, tore it up and thrust it into the wastepaper basket under his table. He muttered, 'Don't come to me for help even if Samuel throttles you. You deserve your Samuel.'

CRACKERS

Sukumar Ray

RAMPADA had brought a pot of sweets to the school on his birthday. As soon as the bell went for the tiffin-break, we shared the sweets amongst ourselves with great enthusiasm. Only Pagla Dashu decided not to have any.

It wasn't as though he did not care for sweets. But there was no love lost between Rampada and him, and the two of them used to quarrel frequently. 'Give Dashu some sweets,' we told Rampada. 'Well, Dashu? Want some?' Rampada said. 'If you're dying for some just tell me, and don't come quarrelling with me again—I'll let you have some sweets.' It would have been natural to be angry on hearing this, but Dashu gravely held his hand out for the sweets, and then proceeded to feed them to the darwan's goat. Then, staring at the pot of sweets for some time, he suddenly began to smile secretly to himself, before walking out of the school. Meanwhile, the rest of us turned to our games after disposing of the sweets—no one had the time to wonder where Dashu had gone.

Back in class after the tiffin-break, we discovered Dashu sitting quietly in a corner, doing sums. I was suspicious at once. 'Have you been up to something, Dashu?' I asked him. 'Yes, I finished two GCM sums,' he answered innocently. 'Who's talking of sums?' I said. 'Are you planning a prank of some kind?' This made him furious. Our teacher, whom we called Pondit Mohashoy, had entered by then, and Dashu was about to complain to him. We mollified Dashu with a great deal of effort and persuaded him to resume his seat.

Pondit Mohashoy wasn't a bad sort. He was seldom in a rush to teach. It was just that he flew into a rage if the class got too noisy. His temper acquired a fine edge when that happened. Taking his seat, Pondit Mohashoy said, 'Recite all the declensions for river,' and promptly fell asleep. Opening our books, we mumbled some gibberish at the tops of our voice, and realized from the beautiful rumbles emanating from Pondit Mohashoy's nostrils that he was deep in slumber by now. So we began to play noughts and crosses, pausing to chant the declensions whenever the rumbling became less loud. We discovered that it worked as miraculously as a lullaby.

All of us were so busy playing that we paid no attention to what Dashu was doing in a corner. A little later something went pffft under Pondit Mohashoy's chair. Frowning in his sleep, he said, 'Uff!' and was about to deliver a scolding when a booming series of explosions shook the entire school. It seemed that all the workmen of the world had gathered on the roof to hammer on it in some grotesque rhythm, or that all the blacksmiths and carpenters in the universe were pounding on it with their tools. For a few minutes we sat there with our mouths open, all of us in a state of what is referred to in the textbooks as discombobulation. Pondit Mohashoy emitted a single, monstrous cry and then, jumping over his desk, his arms and legs flailing, collapsed in a heap on the floor in the middle of the classroom. Not even Nabin Pal from the government college, who always won the gold medal for the high jump, had ever leapt so high. Students from the class below ours had been reciting the tables loudly in the next room—they, too, froze in fear. In no time at all there was utter pandemonium all over the school—even the darwan's dog became flustered and added to the turmoil with high-pitched yelps.

When things grew quieter after about five minutes of explosions, Pondit Mohashoy said, 'Find out what that was.' Darwan-ji used a long bamboo pole to gingerly prod at an earthen pot beneath the chair, pushing it into everyone's view. It was the pot in which Rampada had brought his sweets, traces of which were still to be seen around its mouth. Scowling, Pondit Mohashoy said, 'Whose pot is that?' Rampada said, 'Mine, sir.' At once he found both his ears being twisted mercilessly. 'What did you have in the pot?' Now Rampada realized that the entire blame was about to descend on him. He quickly tried to explain, 'I brought sweets in it, sir, and then ...' Before he could finish, Pondit Mohashoy said, 'And the sweets turned into crackers and began to explode, didn't they?' This was followed by resounding slaps.

Several other teachers had gathered. They ganged up too and bore down on Rampada. We realized it was a dire situation.

Rampada was about to be beaten up for no fault of his. Meanwhile Dashu took my notebook and displayed it to Pondit Mohashoy, saying, 'Look, sir, they were playing noughts and crosses while you were asleep.' Since the notebook had my name on it, Pondit Mohashoy lifted his hand to slap me but suddenly stopped in confusion. Glaring at Dashu, he said, 'Quiet! Who said I was asleep?' Staring at him in consternation, Dashu said, 'But you were snoring.' Swiftly changing the subject, Pondit Mohashoy said, 'So all of them were playing, were they? And what were you doing?' Dashu answered nonchalantly, 'I was lighting the crackers.' We were astounded. What on earth was he saying?

For about half a minute no one spoke. Then Pondit Mohashoy roared, 'Why were you lighting the crackers?' Dashu wasn't to be intimidated. Pointing to Rampada, he said, 'Why didn't he want to give me his sweets to eat?' Rampada responded to this peculiar piece of logic with, 'They're my sweets, I'll do what I please with them.' At once Dashu said, 'Then they're my crackers, I'll do what I please with them.' You can't argue with a mad man. The teachers scolded him and went back to their respective classrooms. Dashu's reputation for being eccentric earned him no punishment.

When school gave out not all our arguments could make Dashu accept that he was at fault. He kept saying, 'My crackers, Rampada's pot. If it's my fault, it's his fault too. He deserved to be beaten up.'

Translated from Bengali by Arunava Sinha

THE HEADMASTER AND THE HORSE

Vinayak Varma

MASILAMANI, the headmaster, reached the village each morning on the 7 a.m. train from the city. It was a twenty-minute walk from the station to the school, past the rice fields and across the river, which got him to the auditorium just as the assembly bell rang.

Once or twice a week, though, Masilamani would take the long route past the temple, so he could stop at Basheer-ikka's idli kadai for a second breakfast of bonda-sambar and filter coffee. 'This is jolly good, Basheer-ikka!' he'd tell the bonda-master every time. 'Jolly good, indeed!'

On these bonda days, the headmaster always missed the morning assembly. He blamed the delay on the Railways. 'Our trains are so unreliable,' he would complain to the other teachers. 'The Railways really need to pull up their socks!' And then he'd giggle wildly at the thought of trains wearing socks.

Today had been one of Masilamani's bonda days, and this time he was late to school by a whole hour. He muttered apologies to no one in particular as he lumbered through the school gates. After four bondas—two more than he was used to eating—his stomach felt rather heavy. He looked forward to flopping into the cane chair in his office for a quick snooze before class.

Masilamani was the kind of nervous walker who kept looking down at his feet instead of at the road ahead. He disliked potholes and slush, hated getting dirt on himself, and was terrified of snakes and frogs, so he watched the ground like a hawk as he walked. He finally took his eyes off his feet and looked up, just as he neared the school's admin block, and saw Janaki Miss and Vengadasalam-thaatha waiting for him by the cycle shed. Masilamani instantly recoiled at the sight of Vengadasalam.

The old peon, an ex-serviceman who was otherwise quite neat, was now coated from head to toe in a gross grey sludge, and sprinkled with all sorts of rubbish. Dry leaves and bits of paper clung to his hair, and a bright yellow toffee-wrapper hung off one of his earlobes.

'Uhhhh,' said the headmaster, his ability to speak having melted away. 'Wha...Huh...Whuh...Buhh...Ehhhhwww.'

'Oh, Mani sir!' cried Vengadasalam, walking towards Masilamani. 'Sir, I'm so glad that you're here at last!'

'NO!' said Masilamani, finding his words at last, and running backwards in horror. 'STAY AWAY FROM ME!'

As he hurtled clear of the peon, Masilamani's heel caught on a tuft of grass that knocked him down. He landed on his bum with a smack and a 'whoomph!'

'Oho! Here, sir,' said Vengadasalam, and stuck out a goo-soaked hand. 'Let me help you up...'

'NO!' yelled Masilamani, scrambling away from Vengadasalam

on all fours like a crab. 'STAND BACK!' The headmaster staggered to his feet, dusted off the seat of his pants, and tried to collect himself.

'WHAT is going on here, Vengy-thaatha?' he asked at length, pointing a shaky finger at the old man. 'Have you been mud-wrestling? How can you come to work looking like this, looking like ... like some GIANT SWAMP TOAD?' The very thought of such a creature made Masilamani shudder.

Vengadasalam began sobbing. 'Oh, Mani sir! I thought that at least YOU would show me some sympathy!' The toffee-wrapper slid down his neck and came to rest on his collar. 'Ayyoo-ho! Ayyoooo-ho! Blub! Wub! Baaa...!'

Janaki Miss, the physics teacher, who had been standing by, watching all of this as if it were a living science experiment, stepped forth. 'Mani sir. Good morning, sir. Please. This ghastly mess is really not Vengy-thaatha's fault...'

'It's really NOT, Mani sir!' Vengadasalam pitched in. 'Blub! That's what I was trying to say! It's the horse's fault, sir! It's the girl's fault, sir!'

'What? Which girl? What horse?' asked Masilamani. ('Am I going mad?' he wondered to himself.)

'The horse in the library, sir!' cried Vengadasalam. 'Ayyoooo-ho! Ohhhh-ho!'

'Eh? The what? In the where?'

'THAT girl, sir!' said Janaki miss, pointing towards the cycle shed.

Masilamani peered into the shed and saw a small, dark shape peering back at him from the shadows, crouched behind the watchman's Hercules Roadster.

'Come here, Thangu,' said Janaki Miss. 'Don't be afraid.'

'I'm NOT afraid!' said a voice that did, in fact, sound rather afraid.

A little girl stepped out of the shed and faced Masilamani with a defiant expression. She had long, unruly hair and big seashell ears, her shirt was half untucked, and a blue canvas school bag hung lopsidedly off her back. Cradled in her arms was an uncommonly large rat. It lay there perfectly still—it was either fast asleep or quite dead.

The headmaster saw the rat and bolted behind Janaki Miss. If there was one thing Masilamani feared more than dirt and reptiles, it was rodents.

'She ... she ... she's carrying a BANDICOOOOOOOOT!' he screamed, the bondas threatening to climb back up his throat.

'It's not a bandicoot,' said the girl. 'It's a RAT!'

'We can deal with the rat later, sir,' said Janaki Miss, calmly. 'First, we must go find the horse. We need to get it out of the school before it creates any more trouble.'

'A horse?' asked Masilamani. 'There's a horse within the school premises?'

'Precisely, sir,' said Janaki Miss. 'Come, I'll show you. Young Thangamani can wait with Vengy-thaatha, meanwhile. Thangu, please stay here. Vengy-thaatha, please make sure the girl doesn't leave.'

'Yes, madam,' said Vengadasalam, and placed a sludgy palm on the girl's head. The girl grinned, not seeming to care that her hair was now streaked with the smelly grey-black slick.

Janaki Miss directed Masilamani towards the main building. He looked relieved at having moved away from the rodent.

'Where are we going?' he asked.

'To the library,' said Janaki Miss.

'But the library is locked,' said Masilamani.

The school's trustees had locked up the library when the river overflowed into the school grounds last year, worried that the books would get damaged by the rising waters. The trustees had moved to the US soon afterwards, taking the library keys with them. The school staff had been too afraid thereafter to call their bosses to ask for permission to break the lock.

'No longer,' said Janaki Miss. 'It's open now.'

'It's open?' asked Masilamani. 'Who unlocked it?'

'Not unlocked, sir. Smashed. The horse did it.'

'The horse?'

'The horse. With one swift kick. You'll see.'

As they turned the corner into the library corridor, they saw, sure enough, that the once-locked library doors were now ajar. A cluster of children crowded the doorway, craning their necks and climbing over each other to catch a view of whatever lay inside.

'CHILDREN!' roared Masilamani, making the kids jump in fright. 'GO TO YOUR CLASSES IMMEDIATELY!'

The headmaster was notorious for making naughty students do maths sums during sports periods. Nobody liked maths. With a panicked shriek and a flutter of hasty footsteps, the crowd was gone.

Masilamani stepped through the library doors and looked around. It was a large room, almost the size of a basketball court, packed with rows and rows of bookshelves. Its windows were still shuttered, so the room was pitch dark except for the dusty rhomboid of sunlight at the doorway.

'Janaki, the switchboard?' he asked.

'Behind the librarian's desk, sir,' said Janaki Miss.

'Good, good. Jolly good.' He found the board and turned on all the lights. 'Wow. I'd forgotten how many books we had in here. I've missed this room.'

'Me too, sir.'

'I suppose we should be thankful to this horse, for giving us our library back,' he said. 'Where IS the horse, by the way? Do you see it?'

'There, sir,' said Janaki Miss, pointing to the far right corner of the room. A pair of white ears peeked over the top of a tall bookshelf in the senior-school reading section. 'There, behind the mythology books.'

'I'd like to know how on earth it got into the building,' said Masilamani. 'And how is the little girl with the rat involved in all this?'

'The watchman saw young Thangamani lead the horse into the grounds, sir. We don't yet know why she did it.'

'And how did it find its way into the library?'

'Well, it's partly my fault, sir. The animal was grazing on the cricket field when I first saw it. I asked Vengy-thaatha to lead it out of the compound, but he decided to ride it out instead.'

'What? He decided to RIDE it? But why?'

'He claims he's had some experience riding horses in his army days.'

'I see.'

'Vengy-thaatha mounted the horse, and spurred it towards the gate. It was all going fine until they got to the cycle shed. That's when little Thangamani returned, carrying that big rat of hers. God only knows where she found it. The horse saw the rat, got scared and galloped off full speed, with Vengy-thaatha hanging on for dear life. It ran straight into the building. Thaatha fell off along the way, right into the waste ditch.'

'Oh no! The poor man!'

'Then the horse came here, kicked open the library door, breaking the lock in the process, and disappeared inside. And now here we are.'

Masilamani took out his handkerchief and wiped the top of his head. 'Okay,' he said. 'Let's go have a look at it.'

They tiptoed towards the senior section. The floor there was covered with books, many of which bore angry hoof-marks.

The horse stood next to the Epics shelf, chewing on Homer's *Collected Works*. It was huge, white and brown, and had long eyelashes and a clipped mane.

'Hello,' Masilamani said.

'Whumfff!' said the horse, and swung its head up and down. 'Whuff-a-whuff-a-whumfff!'

Masilamani stepped back a few paces.

'Do you think it'll bite if I try to touch it?' whispered Masilamani.

'It might, sir,' Janaki Miss whispered back.

'Best not to, then.'

'Yes, sir.'

'Okay. Here's the plan. You know the bridge near the old banyan? There's a nice, empty field next to it. The horse can graze there. We need to take it there.'

'But how do we lead it out, sir?'

'Do you know if we have any carrots in the school, Janaki?'

'Why carrots, sir?'

'I've read somewhere that horses like carrots.'

'No harm in trying. I'll check in the staff kitchen.'

'Jolly good. Jolly good.'

Half an hour later, Masilamani was back in the library, a large carrot in hand. He walked over to the horse.

'Cluck-cluck-cluck,' he said, holding out the carrot. 'Tut-tut-tut.'

The horse looked at Masilamani and snorted. Masilamani wiped the sweat off his forehead and moved closer.

'Come here, horsie!' he said, through clenched teeth. 'Thu-thu-thu-thu. Here's a nice carrot for you, horsie! Chk-chk-chk-chk. Shh-shhh-shhh-shhh!'

The shushing sound seemed to have some effect on the horse. It slowly stepped forward.

'Shh-shh-shhh-shhhh!' said Masilamani, and started making his way towards the door, still holding out the carrot.

The horse followed him.

Shivering with a mixture of fear and triumph, Masilamani shuffled through the doors and into the corridor.

'Shh-shh-shh-shh-shhhhh!'

The horse followed him.

Masilamani walked out onto the field, gaining in courage, picking up speed.

'Shhhhh-shh-shh-shhhhh-shhhh-shh!'

The horse followed.

Janaki Miss, Vengadasalam, Thangamani and the rat watched the little procession from the cycle shed. The rest of the schoolchildren looked out through their classroom windows, babbling with excitement.

The headmaster smiled, waved at everyone, and walked out the gate, carrot in hand, horse in tow.

'Shhhhh-shh-shh-shhhhh-shhhh-shh!'

And they both disappeared down the road. The whole school cheered and clapped.

When Masilamani returned a few minutes later, he had a big smile on his face. He was still holding the carrot.

'What happened, sir?' asked Janaki Miss. 'The horse didn't eat it?'

'I don't think it wanted the carrot,' said Masilamani. 'As soon as it saw the bridge, it ran off down the road like it was being chased by the devil himself.'

'How odd,' said Janaki Miss.

'Maybe the bridge reminded the horse of its way home. I'm jolly glad it's gone, either way. Jolly glad.'

'Me too, Mani sir,' said Vengy-thaatha, wincing.

'Poor old Vengy-thaatha,' said Masilamani. 'Please go home and have a bath, thaatha. And don't come back. Take an extra day off, if you need to.'

'Thank you, Mani sir!' said Vengy-thaatha, stepping forward to shake the headmaster's hand. 'Thank you very much!'

'No! NO, VENGY-THAATHA! NO TOUCHING! You NEED a BATH first! PLEASE! GO HOME, thaatha!'

'Okay, okay. Habba! Okay! I'm going, sir.'

'Now,' said Masilamani, turning to Thangamani. 'What about our little animal-lover here? What's your name, child?'

'Thangamani, sir,' said Thangamani.

'Which class are you in?'

'Class Three, sir. B-section.'

'Okay, Thangamani of Class 3B,' said Masilamani. 'Please get rid of that dirty rat and come to my office. I want an explanation for what happened today. Janaki Miss, you may return to your class.'

'NO, I WON'T! This is MY rat!' said Thangamani. The shouting startled the rat. It began wiggling around feverishly in the girl's arms.

'Are you sure you don't want me to stick around, sir?' asked Janaki Miss, looking at the rat with some concern.

'I can handle this,' said Masilamani, who had found new courage after the horse incident. 'You may carry on, Janaki. Young Thangamani, please come with me.'

Thangamani didn't move. She clutched the rat harder.

'Don't be scared,' said Masilamani, smiling and waving the carrot in the air. 'I promise not to make you do any sums today. Come. I only want to talk.'

The rat seemed to suddenly see the carrot for the first time. It leapt out of Thangamani's arms and onto Masilamani, who screamed and threw the carrot into a row of bushes next to the shed. The rat scurried over Masilamani's head, down his back and ran off into the bushes after the carrot.

'I've had enough of this nonsense! You will come to the office NOW, child!' said Masilamani, and strode into the building in a huff. The girl followed, grinning.

At his office, the headmaster flung himself into his favourite cane chair with a great sigh, and beckoned to Thangamani to sit down.

'Tell me, Thangamani,' said Masilamani. 'Why did you bring that horse into our school?'

'I didn't, sir,' said Thangamani, scowling.

'If you tell me the truth, I'll let you go home early today.'

'REALLY, sir?'

'REEAALLLY! Did you bring the horse here? Tell me the truth.'

'Okay, I brought the horse.'

'Why? And where did you find it?'

'I LIKE horses, sir. I found it in a field.'

'Hmm. And the rat?'

'I LIKE rats, sir.'

'Hmm. You like horses, and you like rats.'

'I also like dogs, and crows, and snails, and foxes, and bears, and frogs, and snakes, and ...'

'Okay, okay, I get it,' said Masilamani, shuddering at the mention of snakes and frogs. 'You know you caused a lot of trouble for us today, don't you?'

'Sir?'

'Poor Vengy-thaatha fell into the waste ditch, the library was ransacked, I was attacked by a rat, and a lot of the school's time was wasted.'

Thangamani grinned. 'Yes, sir,' she said. 'I know all that, sir. But I also got the library reopened, didn't I, sir?'

Masilamani sighed again. 'Look, I know I promised not to give you sums to do, and I promised to send you home early. I'll keep my word. But I'm going to have to tell your parents about all this. Do you understand?'

'You can't, sir.'

'I can't what?'

Thangamani stood up and leaned forward. 'Call my parents, sir. I won't let you!'

Masilamani frowned. 'You won't LET me? I'm your headmaster, child. I can call them whenever I wish!'

'Sir, if you call my parents, I'll tell all the teachers about YOUR little secret.'

'What? What secret?'

'I know why you come late to school every week, sir. I know it's not because of the train. I know all about the bondas, sir.'

Masilamani turned tomato-chutney-red. 'What! How do you know about that?'

'You go to Basheer-ikka's idli kadai, don't you, sir?'

'This is blackmail, child!'

'Yes, sir.'

'Who else knows about this?' he asked.

'Only me and my parents, sir.'

'What? Your PARENTS know? How?'

'Well, sir, Basheer-ikka is my father.'

Masilamani stared at Thangamani in silence. Thangamani stared back.

The strangeness of the day suddenly caught up with the headmaster, and he began shaking uncontrollably.

'Hnnnn,' he said. 'Hnnnn. Hnnnn. Hrrrnnnn.'

Thangamani looked at the headmaster nervously. ('Is he going mad?' she wondered to herself.)

Masilamani shook back and forth, again and again. Then he erupted with laughter.

'Hahahahahaha! HRRRRR! HAHAHAHAHAHAHA!

Basheer's daughter! Hahahaha! Oh, you little brat! BAHAHAHAHAHAHA!'

Thangamani grinned.

'Go home!' said Masilamani. 'Go, before I change my mind and call your parents!'

'Thank you, sir,' said Thangamani, picking up her bag and walking to the door. 'I'll bring you some bondas tomorrow, sir. That way you don't have to be late to school!'

'Hahaha. A good plan. Jolly good,' said Masilamani, his stomach already rumbling. 'Jolly good, indeed.'

UNCLES, AUNTS AND OTHER MISCHIEF- MAKERS

MISCHIEF MANAGED

Paro Anand

SHIVI and Gogo were worried. And sad. And puzzled.

Dada and Dadi had always been so loving. They loved everyone, especially Shivi and Gogo, their grandchildren. And they especially loved each other. They always listened to what the other was saying and even if they didn't agree, they would disagree lovingly and logically.

But, for the past month, things had changed. They always seemed to be cross and fighting.

To the cook they would say, 'You've been working here for fifteen years, when will you learn to cook?'

To Shivi, 'Why don't you stop looking at that stupid phone of yours and do something useful with your life?'

To Gogo, 'Why must you always leave your things lying around? Tidy up!'

Sometimes it was Dada and sometimes it was Dadi. But

they both had frowny faces all the time, instead of their usual smiley ones.

And the worst of it was when it came to talking to each other.

'Why didn't you wake me for my walk this morning?'

'Why don't you set your own alarm clock?'

'I did, but I finally went to sleep after tossing and turning all night from your snoring.'

'*My* snoring? Have you heard yourself? Oh sorry, how could you, you're totally deaf.'

'Arre, it's you who have made me deaf after years of listening to you shrieking like a shrew.'

'What's a shrew?' asked Gogo, but Shivi didn't know. Of course they knew it couldn't be anything very nice. What they did know was that they had to do something about it.

'But what?'

Shivi tried talking to Dada, Gogo tried playing with Dadi, but nothing seemed to make it better.

That night, both boys lay awake. They had both got BIG scoldings from their grandparents although they had been on their best behaviour. Even Papa and Mummy had got BIG scoldings.

'Gogo, psst … let's sneak into Dada Dadi's room tonight after they've gone to sleep.'

'And do what, get another scolding?'

'I don't know, but I think we've got to try.'

So, both boys got out of bed and crept to the door. They looked left and right, making sure no one was awake. But the house only rang with snores coming from all the grown-ups' rooms. Which made Gogo giggle.

'Shhh!' warned Shivi. Their mother was a very light sleeper and would put an end to their adventure in a minute if she heard them. Gogo put his hand over his mouth to stop any sound coming out. The unspent laughter shook his shoulders. Shivi waited till he had finished his laughs and then Shivi and Gogo crept into Dada Dadi's room on tiptoe. Moonlight streamed in from the open window, so the boys could see where they were going.

'Humph prumphf ...' went Dada

'Mmumphrephu,' went Dadi.

They were both still fighting. Even in their sleep. Their frowns were still in place on their faces. They were facing each other as though ready to do battle. But no words came out clearly because both their mouths were sunk in. They weren't wearing their teeth.

Actually, they looked kind of funny. And although Shivi was dying to laugh himself, he shot a warning look at his brother.

The boys looked around. They didn't know what to do.

Shivi pointed at the bathroom door and in they crept. The light was on and, immediately, both boys saw the same thing.

On the counter above the sink stood two glasses of water with Dada and Dadi's dentures swimming in each one.

'Shivi, look ...'

'Yes, both sets of teeth seem to be smiling at each other now. But as soon as they are in their mouths, Dada Dadi start snapping at each other.'

'Do you think ...'

'That the teeth ...'

'Are in the wrong mouths?'

Now both of them dissolved into fits of giggles.

Then, very quietly, Shivi picked up Dada's dentures and Gogo fished out Dadi's. They switched the dentures. Shivi put Dada's teeth into Dadi's glass and Gogo put Dadi's teeth into Dada's glass. It seemed to boys that the teeth were smiling more broadly now. High fiving, Shivi said, 'I bet if they could they would wink at us.'

Next morning Shivi and Gogo were up early, dressed and ready for school. That's when Dada came out of their room. His frown had melted, his teeth shone brightly. He called out to Dadi behind him, 'Dearest, you sleep, let me bring you tea in bed.'

Next moment, Dadi came out, fairly skipping, 'No, no, it is I who should bring you your tea in bed. I must have kept you awake with the snoring. You go rest.'

They were soon giggling like happy little children as they poured each other's tea. Then they turned to their grandsons, giving them a shiny, bright smile each.

Shivi and Gogo glanced at one another. They high fived again.

'Mischief managed,' whispered Shivi under his breath, as Gogo laughed. They were big Harry Potter fans, after all.

GRANDFATHER'S MANY FACES

Ruskin Bond

GRANDFATHER had many gifts, but perhaps the most unusual—and at times startling—was his ability to disguise himself and take on the persona of another person, often a street vendor or carpenter or washerman; someone he had seen around for some time, and whose habits and characteristics he had studied.

His normal attire was that of an average Anglo-indian or Englishman—bush shirt, khaki shorts, occasionally a sola topi or sun helmet—but if you rummaged through his cupboards, you would find a strange assortment of garments: dhotis, lungis, pyjamas, embroidered shirts and colourful turbans. He could be a maharaja one day, a beggar the next. Yes, he even had a brass begging bowl, but he used it only once, just to see if he could pass himself off as a bent-double beggar hobbling through the bazaar. He wasn't recognized, but he had to admit that begging was a most difficult art.

'You have to be on the street all day and in all weathers,' he told me that day. 'You have to be polite to everyone—no beggar succeeds by being rude! You have to be alert at all times. It's hard work, believe me. I wouldn't advise anyone to take up begging as a profession.'

Grandfather really liked to get the 'feel' of someone else's occupation or lifestyle. And he enjoyed playing tricks on his friends and relatives.

Grandmother loved bargaining with shopkeepers and vendors of all kinds. She would boast that she could get the better of most men when it came to haggling over the price of onions or cloth or baskets or buttons … Until one day the sabziwalla, a wandering vegetable seller who carried a basket of fruit and vegetables on his head, spent an hour on the verandah arguing with Granny over the price of various items before finally selling her what she wanted.

Later that day, Grandfather confronted Granny and insisted on knowing why she had paid extra for tomatoes and green chillies. 'Far more than you'd have paid in the bazaar,' he said.

'How do you know what I paid him?' asked Granny.

'Because here's the ten-rupee note you gave me,' said Grandfather handing back her money. 'I changed into something suitable and borrowed the sabziwalla's basket for an hour!'

Grandfather never used make-up. He had a healthy tan and with the help of a false moustache or beard, and a change of hairstyle, he could become anyone he wanted to be.

One winter the Gemini circus came to our small north Indian town and set up its tents on the old Parade Ground. Grandfather, who liked circuses and circus people, soon made friends with all the show folk—the owner, the ringmaster, the lion tamer, the pony riders, clowns, trapeze artists and acrobats. He told me that as a boy he had always wanted to join a circus, preferably as an animal trainer or ringmaster, but his parents has persuaded him to become an engine driver instead.

'Driving an engine must be fun,' I said.

'Yes, but lions are safer,' said Grandfather.

And he used his friendship with the circus folk to get free passes for me, my cousin Melanie, and my small friend Gautam, who lived next door.

'Aren't you coming with us?' I asked Grandfather.

'I'll be there,' he said. 'I'll be with my friends. See if you can spot me!'

We were convinced that Grandfather was going to adopt one of his disguises and take part in the evening's entertainment. So for Melanie, Gautam and me the evening turned out to be a guessing game.

We were enthralled by the show's highlights—the tigers going through their drill, the beautiful young men and women on the flying trapeze, the daring motorcyclist bursting through a hoop of fire, the jugglers and clowns—but we kept trying to see if we could recognize Grandfather among the performers. We couldn't make too much noise because in the row behind us sat some of the town's senior citizens—the mayor, a turbaned maharaja, a formally dressed Englishman with a military bearing, a couple of nuns and Gautam's class teacher! But we kept up our chatter for most of the show.

'Is your Grandfather the lion tamer?' asked Gautam.

'I don't think so,' I said. 'He hasn't had any practice with lions. He's better with tigers!' But there was someone else in charge of the tigers.

'He could be one of the jugglers,' said Melanie.

'He's taller than the jugglers,' I said.

Gautam made an inspired guess: 'Maybe he's the bearded lady!'

We looked hard and long at the bearded lady when she came to our side of the ring. She waved to us in a friendly manner, and Gautam called out, 'Excuse me, are you Ruskin's grandfather?'

'No, dear,' she replied with a deep laugh. 'I'm his girlfriend!' And she skipped away to another part of the ring.

A clown came up to us and made funny faces.

'Are *you* Grandfather?' asked Melanie.

But he just grinned, somersaulted backwards, and went about his funny business.

'I give up,' said Melanie. 'Unless he's the dancing bear…'

'It's a *real* bear,' said Gautam. 'Just look at those claws!'

The bear looked real enough. So did the lion, though a trifle mangy. And the tigers looked tigerish.

We went home convinced that Grandfather hadn't been there at all.

'So, did you enjoy the circus?' he asked, when we sat down to dinner later that evening.

'Yes, but you weren't there,' I complained. 'And we took a close look at everyone—including the bearded lady!'

'Oh, I was there all right,' said Grandfather. 'I was sitting right behind you. But you were too absorbed in the circus to notice the audience. I was that smart-looking Englishman in suit and tie, sitting between the maharaja and the nuns. I thought I'd just be myself for a change!'

THE BOY WHO COULDN'T WAIT

Shruthi Rao

VENKI Mama was one cool uncle.

For one, he wore bell-bottom trousers, like the filmstars.

'Your legs look like they're wearing skirts,' grumbled Ajji.

'Fashion, Amma,' said Venki Mama.

'There's enough cloth around your ankles to stitch another pair of trousers,' said Ajja.

'Enough for a pair of bell-bottoms for me?' wondered Raghu, with longing. But didn't dare ask.

Venki Mama presided over 'Headquarters'—which was what Raghu's father called the grand old house belonging to Ajji-Ajja, Raghu's maternal grandparents. It was in a village with farmlands all around and plenty of places to play. This was where all the grandchildren of Ajji-Ajja spent their summer vacations. For two months, Venki Mama was the Pied Piper to his nieces and nephews.

And as if to underscore how cool he was, Venki Mama had just installed a shower in the bathroom. Behind the bathroom was the cowshed, and the outer wall of the bathroom had a tap for cowshed-related use. Venki Mama had cleverly added an attachment and drawn another pipe from there to the bathroom. To the end of the pipe, he fixed an old tin can with holes in it, and that served as the shower-head.

Venki Mama operated the lever next to the shower-head to control the water flow. Raghu gazed open-mouthed—the spray felt like rain on his outstretched fingers.

'Please can I use the shower tomorrow?' begged Raghu.

'We'll see,' said Venki Mama. 'Next month, perhaps, if you've been on good behaviour.'

Raghu pouted. Ajji, who was passing by, stroked Raghu's cheeks. 'Why worry? This shower-thing sprays only cold water, and the water stops the moment the cowshed tap is turned on. Useless. A nice hot bucket bath is not good enough for this Venki. What fancies the young people of these days have! In our time …'

But Raghu was distracted as Venki Mama nonchalantly fished out a comb from the back pocket of his pants and ran it through his forelocks in one single, elegant sweep backwards. Raghu sighed. What style! He must try it out when nobody was looking.

'Let's go to the river, Venki Mama!' said Raghu.

'Adults don't have summer vacations,' said Venki Mama. 'I have work in the market. I'll be back by lunch.'

Venki Mama away at work. Amma busy with Ajji. Ajja in his office. And one whole day until his cousins arrived. Ugh! What would Raghu do all alone?

He darted in and out of the rooms. He bounced on rolled-up mattresses. He tried to clamber onto the tiled roof. He hurtled into the kitchen and almost ran into the pot of huli boiling on the stove—and was shouted at by Ajji. He stuck his fingers in a jar of mango pickle—and had his wrist thwacked by Amma. He swung like a monkey on the line of washing in the backyard and was scolded by Ajja.

He peered into the well. He used to have so much fun, throwing things into the well, counting the seconds they took to fall. Observing how fast each object sunk. Tricking his younger cousins to toss things in and then watching them get into trouble. Tch. They had installed a meshed door now on the mouth of the well, with a lock and everything. He contented himself with pushing in sticks and stones into the gaps in the wire mesh. Not as much fun. Oh what-oh-what could he do?

Lunchtime finally came around, and with it, Venki Mama. Raghu wolfed down the heap of steaming rice on his banana leaf topped with halasinakayi huli. He demanded more pieces of the raw jackfruit until he felt sure his belly would burst. He could barely finish the curd-rice with the pickle that he had tried to pilfer earlier.

The moment Venki Mama finished his last morsel, Raghu was upon him. 'The river, Venki Mama, now!'

'Too hot,' said Venki Mama, scratching his belly and yawning loudly.

'It's not!' said Raghu. 'There are trees next to the river, it'll be shady, let's go.'

'Tell you what,' said Venki Mama. 'I'll take a nap now. You can wake me up at four, and I'll take you to the river.'

Four! Raghu glanced at the clock that hung just outside the kitchen. It was only one-thirty now!

Within moments, the house was cloaked in silence.

'You come and sleep too, Raghu,' called Ajji.

'Raghu? An afternoon nap? High hopes,' said Amma.

Raghu lay down next to Ajji just to defy Amma. But he couldn't sleep. He got up. He briefly considered going to the river on his own. But it was across the highway, and he knew how rashly the bus-drivers drove.

He twiddled his thumbs. He counted the rafters. He followed ants to their home and destroyed it. He looked at the clock. He watched the cows chew cud. He tried to tickle one with a stalk of hay. It snorted, and he fell backwards in alarm. He looked at the clock. He climbed the cashewnut tree. He skinned his knee. He looked at the clock. Still two-thirty! He watched the clouds. He cursed his aunts for not arriving today itself and bringing his cousins. He looked at the clock. 2:45. Ughhh, if only he could make the hands of the clock move faster …

Brilliant idea.

Raghu found a tall stool and half-carried, half-dragged it to the clock. He stood on it, opened the glass covering of the clock, which swung outwards on hinges—and moved the hands of the clock to 4. They moved quite easily, with a pleasing click–click sound.

Job completed, Raghu knocked on Venki Mama's room. 'Mama! Mama! It's four!'

With a lot of grumbling and 'So soon?' Venki Mama came to the door.

Raghu dutifully pointed to the clock, and Venki Mama peered at it sleepily. He rubbed his eyes, and glanced at the shaft of light coming in through an open window. He frowned, ducked into his room, and came back with a small square box, which he opened.

A watch! Wow! Venki Mama had a … uh oh!

Venki Mama looked at the watch, and then at Raghu's face. Raghu's cheeks burned.

'Smart,' said Venki Mama. 'But not smart enough. Also, patience is more important than smartness. No river for you today. You'll have to wait until tomorrow.'

Raghu was hair-tearingly, skin-scratchingly, foot-stompingly disappointed. How could Venki Mama be so unkind? And lazy too! Wasn't sleeping at night enough? Why did he have to sleep in the afternoon too?

The evening stretched interminably before Raghu. Oh for the river and its coolness! How good it would feel to sit on the rock, his feet dangling in the water, the fish nipping at his toes. He could practice stone-skimming, or perhaps shed his clothes and take a dip …

By dinnertime, Raghu was so annoyed that Venki Mama's legs did indeed look like they were wearing skirts.

He was so angry that he was sure he wouldn't be able to fall asleep. But the moment Raghu put his head on his pillow, he felt himself drift away, the images floating in and out as his eyelids closed by themselves. The last thing he heard was chuckling as the adults in the next room talked about Raghu and the clock … but they didn't sound angry, so maybe he was dreaming …

The next morning, Raghu woke up with the bitter taste of disappointment still on his tongue. He went to the bathroom to brush his teeth. As he approached, he heard a soft sprinkling. The shower! Raghu listened at the door. Venki Mama was humming. The water flow decreased, and Raghu heard hearty slaps and sploshes as Venki Mama soaped himself. Raghu paused. His mother and grandmother were in the kitchen. His grandfather was nowhere to be seen. Raghu made the decision in a split second. He ran outside, turned the cowshed tap on, and ducked behind the cowshed. That should serve Venki Mama right.

At once, Venki Mama bellowed. 'Who turned on the cowshed tap? Turn it off! I have soap in my eyes!'

Ajja bellowed. 'Who turned on the cowshed tap? Why is there no bucket to hold the water?'

Ajji bellowed, 'In our time, we used to travel one kilometre to the river to carry back three pots of water! The kids of these days are so used to the luxury of running water that they don't even know the value of …'

Amma turned off the cowshed tap and immediately all the shouting stopped.

In the silence, she bellowed—'Raghuuuuu!!!'

How did she know? She always knew!

She found him. There was that look in her eyes that indicated severe punishment, or worse, a long lecture. 'I've had enough of your mischief!' she began. 'You—'

Just then a bullock-cart trundled into the yard.

Saved!

'They're here!' Amma called towards the kitchen. 'As for you,' she said, turning to Raghu. 'Stay out of troub—oh why do I even bother?'

Raghu had already rushed out to greet his cousins.

The holidays had well and truly begun.

GRANNY TWO

Khyrunnisa A.

'THEY may be ill, they may be well, but having grandparents is truly swell,' said Deepak, opening his smart, much-admired new bag to take out his lunch box. The bag was a present on his last birthday from his grandparents.

'You bet! It's truly yummy to have a grand mummy!' mumbled Suresh, savouring the lunch his grandmother had packed for him, jaws working like a well-oiled machine.

Lunch interval was the time when the boys of Class VII discussed any topic under the sun and that day they had stumbled upon the topic of grandparents. This had happened when Vimal explained to them that he had been late to school because his grandmother had had a fall in the morning and had to be rushed to hospital.

'My grandma is so cool! She's certainly no fool!' Abraham grinned. Everyone knew he got his test papers signed by his fond grandmother who never even glanced at his marks.

'It's definitely not bad to have a generous granddad,' said Arun, caressing his watch, a gift from his grandfather, as he joined in the rhyming game.

'A grandparent is never a tyrant,' contributed Rohan.

'Then listen to this, guys, and don't look any further, there's nothing like having a great-grandmother,' sang Amit.

'Doesn't rhyme, doesn't rhyme!' protested Suresh. 'You should say great grandmurther.'

'What do you mean, great grandmother? Is your grandmother a great person?' asked Abraham. 'Ashoka the Great, Akbar the Great, Peter the Great, Amit's Grandmother the Great!'

'Very funny. Laugh away, but I *was* talking about my grandmother's mother,' Amit retorted.

'What? Grandmother's mother? You must be joking,' Arun raised his eyebrows as the rest looked in disbelief at Amit.

This was just the reaction Amit had hoped to get. Having earned their complete attention, Amit explained, 'Believe it or not, I do have a GREAT-GRANDMOTHER, okay? And next week she's coming here with my grandmother for her birthday. My great-grandmother's birthday, not my grandmother's,' he clarified.

'Swag!' Suresh exclaimed, quite fascinated. 'That's indeed great, man! Is she turning hundred?'

'Not exactly, but she's pretty close to a century. She's coming for her ninetieth birthday.'

Amit lapped up the oohs and the aahs, the wows and the whistles, grinning from ear to ear as the boys gazed at him with new respect and awe, as if he somehow had a role to play in his great-grandmother's astonishing feat.

During the Biology period that afternoon, while their teacher waxed eloquent on the life cycle of the cockroach, Suresh interrupted him to ask if there could be four generations of cockroaches living at the same time. The teacher banged his book shut in exasperation and called it a day, shaking his head and muttering as he left the class, 'What is this generation coming to?'

The following week, Amit invited Suresh and Deepak, his close friends, to his house for his great-grandmother's birthday. The boys were thrilled with the invitation. Ever since they had heard about Amit's unique and antique relation, their interest had been roused and they had been trying hard to wangle an invitation to see her.

'If you call your grandmother Granny, what do you call your great-grandmother?' asked Suresh.

'Oh, I call her Granny too,' said Amit.

'Granny Two? Awesome!' Suresh commented.

The birthday was on Saturday evening and that morning both the boys broached the subject of presents in their respective homes. Deepak's mother suggested a shawl. 'It makes a woman of that age look dignified while keeping her nice and warm,' she said with a wise air.

Suresh's parents felt a walking stick would be quite appropriate and useful. 'People that old need a prop, if they aren't bedridden, of course,' his father opined.

Armed with these gifts the boys met at the bus stop and proceeded to Amit's house. Though the party was at six, they had decided to go a little early to satisfy their curiosity.

They got off at the bus stop that was a kilometre from Amit's house and walked with eager steps to their destination.

'I feel so excited!' said Suresh. 'I'm actually going to meet Granny Two! Amit never told us much about her. Do you think she can walk? I hope so. My gift would go for a six if she's in a wheelchair. Look! I've got a walking stick for her, my mother chose a lovely, light one.' He twirled the gift-wrapped stick with the expertise of a conjuror. He had been practising with the stick from the time it was brought home until his mother took it away. She handed the present, now gift-wrapped, to him only when he was about to set out. 'What are you giving her?'

'I have a pretty silk shawl for her. My parents bought it. It's light too. They said a ninety-year-old feels the cold more severely than a younger person. But it's a dull brown.' Deepak made a face. 'I wanted a nice, bright red, but they said this colour would suit the elderly. What's wrong with ancient people wearing red? I hope Granny Two likes it.'

'I think they are pretty useful gifts, she should like them,' Suresh consoled him.

'If she can see, and talk and hear, that is. Do you think she can?' Deepak looked anxious.

'I have my doubts,' Suresh frowned. 'Maybe she's not right in the head too. That explains why Amit never told us about her.'

They reached the house at five and rang the doorbell. A slightly built lady with twinkling eyes that shone behind her glasses opened the door. Her black hair with streaks of grey running through was tied in a neat knot at the back and she was wearing a loose, flowing salwar kurta.

'Er ... Amit's granny?' asked Suresh.

'Yes, yes, come in, you must be Amit's friends. He's always talking about you. He's gone to the station with his father to pick up his aunt and uncle who are arriving by the five-thirty train. You boys make yourselves comfortable.'

'Where's Aunty? Hope she isn't ill again?' asked Deepak. Amit's mother was always unwell.

'Who? Amit's mother? Poor dear, she's got a temperature and is lying down.'

'Granny Two?' asked Suresh.

'Yes, she's sleeping. She's not yet fully recovered after our long train journey. She has severe arthritis you see, and a bad back.'

'What about our presents? Shall we give them to her?'

'To her? Oh, not now, boys, I think she's asleep. But how very sweet of you!'

The boys' faces fell. 'Can't we just take a look at her, Granny?' Suresh pleaded. 'We won't disturb her. Please.'

'We've been longing to see a really old woman,' Deepak blurted out. 'This is our only chance. We have to tell our friends.'

Granny smiled. 'I don't want to disappoint you. Let me see if she's up.' She opened the door to a room on the side and went in. Strange sounds from within startled the boys. A little later she returned.

'She's fast asleep. You can take the presents and keep them in her room, but don't wake her up. You can give them at the party. Now go inside and see her, but don't linger too long there. And close the door shut when you come out.' She sniffed. 'Oooh! I think something's beginning to burn!' She trotted off to the kitchen.

The boys tiptoed into the room. The peculiar noise was now louder and was coming from the huge bed in the centre. The boys were drawn to the bed, as if it was a magnet pulling them towards it. A fat old lady with white, straggly hair was lying on it, fast asleep, mouth wide open. The boys gazed at her huge frame and listened, fascinated, to her breathing that, coupled with her snoring, produced the bizarre sound they had heard earlier. They felt completely overawed in the presence of a nonagenarian.

'She does look a little like Aunty, doesn't she?' observed Suresh in a hushed undertone, scrutinizing her from north to south, west to east. 'A cinemascope version.'

'See! Look! See!' hissed Deepak, pointing with his finger. 'Her teeth!'

On the bedside in a transparent cup half filled with water were her dentures grinning ghoulishly at the boys. The cup was flanked by her thick glasses on one side and her hearing aid on the other.

'Her specs! Her ear phones! And look, her false hair!' Suresh almost screamed with joy on seeing a hairpiece coiled like a grey snake in one corner of the table. This was more than they had bargained for. The boys could hardly contain their excitement at being privy to this unusual spectacle. With great reverence, they walked around the bed twice as the lady, completely oblivious to the fact that she was being given the attention reserved for a prize exhibit, slept. An exceptionally loud snore-cum-wheeze made them jump. They gazed some more before placing the presents on the table next to the hair piece. With great reluctance, they dragged themselves away from the scene, closed the door and headed for the kitchen.

'What are you making?' they asked Granny who was stirring something on the fire. 'Did anything get burnt?'

'No, I was on time. This is kheer. I've already baked two kinds of cakes. One, a normal chocolate cake and another without much sugar. Amit's mother is diabetic, you know.'

'Granny Two?' asked Suresh.

'Yes, she's also diabetic. And has high blood pressure. So I had to prepare different types of food. Here, have some kheer.'

'Oh, thanks, Granny. This is lovely. You're a great cook.'

The boys felt Granny was a great friend they had known all their lives and began talking to her without any inhibitions.

'Listen, Granny, how do you think it must feel, being so old?' asked Deepak in a confidential manner.

'Okay, I guess,' Granny replied, dimpling.

'What okay, Granny? Granny Two is ninety today. Do you think she'll score a century?'

A mischievous smile lit Granny's face. 'Maybe, with some luck, if she scores in singles.'

The boys laughed.

'But I'm sure when the time comes, you'll reach that landmark, Granny, and in boundaries,' said Suresh kindly.

As Granny laughed her tinkling laugh, they heard the door open and almost immediately Amit's uncle and aunt entered the kitchen. Going straight to Granny, they hugged her in turn, saying, 'Happy birthday, Granny! You look wonderful!'

'What!' exclaimed the boys, jaws dropping in astonishment.

Granny smiled and said, 'Yes, I'm Amit's great-grandmother.' Turning to Amit who had entered the room, she explained, 'They thought your Granny was me. And,' she laughed, 'I let them believe that.'

'Ha, ha, idiots!' said Amit, looking with pride at his great-grandmother. 'My naughty Granny!'

'But why did you say Granny too is ninety?' asked Granny. 'I didn't understand.'

'Er ... we thought Amit said he calls his grandmother "Granny" and his great-grandmother "Granny Two"—like "Volume One" and "Volume Two",' explained Suresh, a little sheepishly.

'You're crazy! I meant I call her Granny too, meaning, I call both Granny,' Amit said.

The room rang with laughter while Suresh and Deepak blushed.

When the cake was cut, Amit's mother wrapped the shawl tightly around her while his grandmother, her hair piece almost falling off, leaned on the walking stick that wobbled in its effort to support her weight. After the cake was cut and everyone sang 'Happy Birthday', Deepak said, 'Three cheers for Granny. You are truly great, Granny!'

'Two!' added the others in a chorus.

MAKING MY OWN BED

Ruskin Bond

WHENEVER a young person asks me for some really serious advice, I say, 'Always make your own bed.' And my young friend goes away laughing, saying, 'Bond-uncle is never serious about anything.'

But I am dead serious. Making one's own bed is a stamp of personality, a statement about being someone different upon this earth, a unique expression of one's individuality. Don't leave it to your mother, sibling or the domestic help; it will become their kind of bed, and you will have to fit your personality to suit theirs.

Apart from that, it can be a matter of self-preservation.

Not so long ago, I was put up in a guest house on the edge of the desert near Jodhpur in Rajasthan. At night I retired to my room. The bed was neatly made. Too neat for my liking. I lifted the pillow and discovered a large black scorpion welcoming me with sting upraised. Well, I am not one to kill any of God's creatures without good reason, and so, using a pencil (they have their uses), I tipped the scorpion into a large plastic mug, opened a window, and deposited the visitor into a flower-bed.

Returning to the bed, I decided upon a little rearrangement of the mattresses, and on lifting one up, discovered an entire nest of scorpions. Disturbed by my interference, scores of young scorpions were soon scampering about on the bedsheets. I made a tactical retreat. The railway station was not far away, and I spent the night on an arm-chair in the station waiting-room. Better a railway bug than a desert scorpion!

* * *

Making my own bed was something I learnt in my school days, when as a boarder, you were at the mercy of prefects, housemasters, and occasional pranksters. You made your own bed, polished your own shoes, and washed behind your ears with Lifebuoy soap. Occasionally, a bright spark would introduce some stinging nettle between your sheets, and you would retaliate in kind, preferably with a spiky cactus. 'French' beds were popular. You rearranged the sheets in such a way that the occupant, getting between them, found himself in a hopeless tangle.

All this meant that you had to be very protective of your own bed. Not only did you make your own bed but you had to guard against all kinds of interlopers.

I became so protective of my bed that when I went to London as a young man and rented a bed-sitting room from a motherly Jewish landlady, I had a regular tussle with her over who had the right to make my bed. She insisted that I was her boarder with a right to sharing the bathroom, and she had a right to tidying my bedroom, including the bed. I would make the bed. She would remake it. I would make it again. Sometimes she won; sometimes I won. In the end we compromised. She would make the bed in the morning, so that I wouldn't be late for work. And in the evenings, when I returned, I could make it again!

When winter came this kind lady produced an old-fashioned stone hot-water bottle, which was most effective. It kept my feet warm all night. As a result I surrendered all bed-making rights to my landlady. A warm bed and a good breakfast, what more can a young man ask for?

Good breakfasts can be had in many of our starred hotels, but I have never really been happy with the beds. For a start, there are far too many pillows. These are flung away before I lie down. How can one sleep propped up like the desiccated corpse in *Psycho*? Then the sheets and blankets have to be loosened, as these are always wedged into the mattress too tightly. Then the mattresses are often too springy and propel you towards the ceiling if you flop on to them suddenly. I have sometimes found it easier to sleep on the floor, using a pillow and blanket from the bed and a thick rug beneath me.

Hotel rooms are very similar to each other, so don't forget your room number. On one occasion I stepped out of my room, leaving the door slightly ajar, to see if there was a stairway at the end of the corridor. (I'm paranoid about lifts and avoid them if I can.) On returning to my room, the door still being open, I found the bed occupied by a large lady in a pink nightdress. I was in the wrong room! Fortunately the lady did not scream, and I backed out, apologizing profusely. She seemed to recognize me, even though she got my name wrong.

'Aren't you that writer fellow, Bunskin Rond?' she asked in good humour. 'Come on in and have a cup of tea.'

It must have been very special tea, a clear golden liquid she was drinking out of a glass. She laughed, and mischief shone in her eyes. She beckoned me closer with a long forefinger.

'Wha-what big nails you have,' I stammered.

'The better to scratch you with, my dear,' she said.

I thought it wise to beat a hasty retreat.

This is why I always say, stick to your own bed and your own bedroom,

Bunskin.

MISCHIEF AMONG FRIENDS

EAU DE COLOGNE FOR THE DOG

Ruskin Bond

WHEN I was a small boy living in Jamnagar on the western coast of India, Ayah was my guardian angel, surrogate mother, friend and beloved all rolled into one and wrapped up in a white sari. My mother, young in years and younger at heart, was often away attending the lunch and tea get-togethers that the ladies of the royal household liked to organize, or she would accompany the younger royals on picnics and excursions. My father spent more time with me, but he would be at work through much of the day. I would be left in the care of the servants. I had no objection to the arrangement, because the servants indulged me. Of them, the one who indulged most of all was Ayah.

She was probably from one of the fishing communities of Kathiawar or from the poorer Muslim families from the north of India who worked in Christian and Anglo-Indian households. She must have been in her thirties and was unusually large and broad-limbed for an Indian woman, and shaped like a papaya. I was told she had a family of her own but I never saw them, and she never spoke of them. She was the one I spent the most time with at home—she stayed all day, washing my clothes, giving me a bath and telling me stories in Hindustani about jinns and fairies and the snake transformed into a handsome prince by the loving touch of a beautiful princess.

Ayah had large, rough hands. She could use those hands very effectively to deliver a few resounding slaps, because I really was a little devil. But her anger vanished as quickly as it came when she saw me break into tears. And then she would break down herself, and cover me with big, wet kisses and gather me into herself. To be hugged and kissed, and generally fussed over, is one of the joys of infancy and childhood. My mother was not a physically demonstrative person—the occasional peck on the cheek was enough emotion for her. But Ayah more than made up for it.

At the time, eau de cologne was the scent of the day, there being nothing else in the shops except something called 'Evening in Paris' which (as I learnt later) was distilled in Aligarh and bottled in Bombay. In the depths of the bazaar you could also pick up little bottles of local perfume—heady stuff, distilled from roses or jasmine, guaranteed to linger on the user for weeks. My mother had a bottle that would sit on her dressing table, and from which she would sprinkle a bit on her hanky and neck before she went out.

Ayah, too, fancied a little eau de cologne from time to time, and I would smuggle the bottle out to her. After sprinkling it over herself, the bottle would be quietly returned to the dressing table. Ayah loved me for this little service. 'A friend for the sake of advantage,' as Aristotle put it!

Came the day when my mother couldn't help noticing the very low level of perfume in the bottle.

'Who's been using my eau de cologne?' demanded mother bear.

'I used it on the dog,' I said quickly, already a good dissembler. 'She was smelling horribly.'

Poor Beauty, our aging Alsatian, did smell a bit but not too badly. However, she was given a good bath in a Dettol solution, and sulked for weeks, not being fond of bathing.

Ayah taught me many things. One of these was the eating of paan. I didn't care for the taste—somewhat bitter, because of the betel nut and lime—but I was fascinated by the red juice, which Ayah would spit with great accuracy in different corners of the overgrown garden. When my parents were out, she would make me a miniature paan—I think she added a little sugar in it—and I would chew the paan and sit in the kitchen, gossiping with her and the cook. Before my parents came home, Ayah would rinse my mouth with warm water, and with her rough fingers she would scrub my teeth clean.

If I swallowed an orange seed, Ayah would say an orange tree would grow inside me. Being an imaginative child, this rather worried me because orange trees, I was told, had thorns on them. I did not want to worry my parents unduly, so I took my problem to Mr Jenkins, who kept a farm nearby. He looked serious, thought about it for a few moments, then said: 'Don't worry, it will only be a small tree.' Still worried, I consulted Osman the cook, who laughed and said, 'Your ayah is just a gapori, don't listen to her.'

'What's a gapori?' I asked.

'One who makes up stories—and exaggerates. Go and tell her you've swallowed a bean.'

I did, and she said, 'Oh, baba, now you'll have a beanstalk growing inside you!'

'And there will be a giant living in it?' I asked.

She burst into laughter, seeing I'd caught her out.

'Osman says you're a gapori,' I told her. And she and Osman had a terrible fight. She chased him around the house and forgave him only when he said he meant she was a pari, a fairy, not a gapori.

Still, I think I learnt something about telling stories from Ayah, as I did from Osman, although I had no idea that I would become a gapori of sorts one day.

THE RECOVERY

Ranjit Lal

TOUSLE-HAIRED ten-year-old Sudha crept into the darkened hospital room, her little heart beating like a bird's. There on that frightening bed, surrounded by tubes and drips, lay her best friend Lalit, his eyes closed, his face pale. Sudha gulped: just imagine, the first words uttered by him when he had regained consciousness after his operation had been, 'Where's Sudha?' Well, she had been by his side when he had collapsed in the park while they were returning home from school. She had cradled his heavy head in her lap until her mother had driven up in response to Sudha's frantic SOS calls. At the hospital, he had been immediately operated upon for an emergency appendectomy.

'How're you feeling? Does it hurt?' she whispered. Lalit's brown eyes flickered.

'Wh ... who are you ... oh Sudha!' He blinked. 'It's okay, I can bear it!' He nodded. Sudha swallowed the huge lump in her throat: why did it seem to hurt her more than it hurt him, she wondered.

'How big is the cut?' she asked. Slowly he opened his arms wide.

'About so big, I think…'

'How many stitches?'

'Dunno, probably over a hundred!'

'You're so brave, Lalit!' She squeezed his hand. 'You know, even in the park you didn't cry.' Actually he had, and had scared the hell out of her.

'I know…' Weakly, he beckoned her close.

'Sudha … can you … can you tell Mom that I would like that remote-controlled helicopter? It would help me get better quickly. And when you come again could you get me some Toblerone?'

She nodded her head vigorously.

'Could I have some water please?' he asked like a soldier dying on a battlefield. Carefully she lifted his head and made him drink a little juice.

'Silly! Don't move!' she admonished, wiping his chin. The room door had opened and his and her mom entered.

'Sweetie, we should leave now; let Lalit rest,' her mother said. Lalit's mom hugged her. 'You're a little angel!' she said, dropping a kiss in her curls.

'Aunty,' Sudha whispered, taking her by the hand and walking towards the door, 'he wants that remote-controlled helicopter. It'll help him get better quickly, he says…'

'Ah, so he does? Well sweetheart, we'll see about that.'

A nurse barged in. 'Uttho baba. Get up and walk!' she ordered, stripping the sheets off the bed and helping Lalit to his feet. She held him up from one side as he put one foot in front of the other, wincing, and walked like a very old man. Sudha quickly held him up by the other.

'You become a nurse too,' the nurse smiled, pinching her cheek. 'Yeh bilkul dhongi hain—this fellow's a complete fraud!'

That evening she brought him his Toblerone and a new super-bouncy ball which she knew he had been eyeing for some time.

'Your mom said "we'll see" about the helicopter,' she reported. 'But I got you this!'

'Thanks,' he whispered, holding the ball in his hands and looking at it sadly. 'I wonder if I'll ever be able to play with it… Sudha … can you open the Toblerone pleaseB…?'

'Sure!' She gave him a piece and took one herself.

'Are you in pain?' she asked. He shook his head and then nodded.

'Sometimes … it's like a red-hot bayonet inside me … but don't worry, I can take it!' He laid back his head on the pillow as if exhausted.

'You're so brave!'

The next morning she went to see him again and met his mom in the corridor.

'I have to see his doctor, darling,' she said and hastened away. Sudha walked up to Lalit's room and paused outside the door, frowning. Strange metallic bangs were coming from inside the room. She put her eye to the keyhole. And gasped: Lalit was standing with his back to the door, a stainless steel bedpan in one hand. With the other he was throwing the bouncy ball at the far wall and then whacking it as it rebounded.

'And that's four!' he yelled and then dived to 'field' the ball as it bounced around the room.

So! Sudha was about to barge in when she paused. Then she knocked. She heard him scamper back to bed, the clang of the bedpan and then a faint weak voice calling, 'Come in.'

'Hi,' she said her eyes bright. 'How're you feeling? Want to walk?'

'Walk? But the nurse isn't here...'

'Doesn't matter, I'm here! Get up now!' Tentatively he stood at the edge of the bed. Sudha picked up the bedpan (screwing up her nose) and ball. She bounced the ball and then hit it towards Lalit.

'*Catch!*' she yelled and instinctively, Lalit stretched his hand out and leapt towards the ball.

'So!' she exclaimed, her arms akimbo.

'Oh-oh!' he grinned sheepishly. And then added pleadingly, 'Sudha, don't tell Mom about this. She'll never buy me that helicopter...'

'Sure, I won't!' Sudha nodded. 'But what's in it for me, mister?'

WHAT A FANTASTIC SHOW!

Subhadra Sen Gupta

'CHARU, hold on! It's tilting again!' Ashish, who was on the stage, muttered frantically from the side of his mouth, his eyeballs rolling in panic.

It was the first act of our Durga Puja play in which all the kids of the area were taking part and disaster had struck early. I was crouched behind the plywood backdrop desperately trying to pull it backwards to stop it from tilting and crashing on to the stage.

On stage the acting was pretty dismal as Ashish and Minnie would say one line of dialogue and glance back nervously at the dangerously swaying set, ready to jump off the stage and into the audience. It was supposed to be a very serious scene about war being declared, but with two jumpy actors saying their dialogues with their backs to the audience, it was only making everyone laugh.

Rahul, our director, squeezing in beside me, whispered wildly, 'Kick it! Kick it!'

We gave the set a few hard kicks, making it slide forward and now it was leaning crazily against the back wall. The fortress that was painted on the set looked like it had been hit by an earthquake. Down in the pandal, the audience gave a joint sigh of relief.

Then from the dark a sarcastic voice said loudly, 'Can we have the scene again please?' And the laughter began.

I crawled back to my prompter's post and picked up the script. Before I began prompting again I said a small prayer to God but He was on leave that day. Then it dawned on me slowly that the words I was reading out and those being spoken on stage did not match. Peering past the corner in the wings where I sat, I could see Minnie mumbling and blinking nervously. All the shocks had made her and Ashish forget their lines and now in desperation they were making them up, mumbling some nonsense. I got as close as I could get to them, crawling right to the edge of the wings and began prompting in the loudest whisper possible.

Our sarcastic friend in the audience spoke again, 'Prompter, quiet!' So now there was more laughter.

I waved frantically to Rahul, 'Pull the curtain down!'

Rahul pulled at the curtain rope, the curtain came down half way and then with a squeak it got stuck. Minnie and Ashish were still ad-libbing away like two lunatics and all the audience could see were their skinny legs.

A new voice spoke from the dark, 'Wow! What's this, an ad for shoes?' More laughter because our comic timing was so good.

Then with a beautiful 'swoosh' the curtain slid down the final inches and the first act was over. I tucked my head into my arms and wished I could go home.

Ashish rushed into the wings and nearly strangled Rahul. 'Can't you even put up a set properly, you idiot! It nearly killed us!'

Minnie turned her wide eyes towards me, 'Charu, what did I say on stage?'

'You should know. You made it up.'

'Oh God!' Minnie prayed.

'God is on leave today.'

'Looks like it.'

Pinky, coming straight from the green room all made up as a Maratha queen, swished in happily. Then she looked at all the red faces and asked, 'Hey! What's the matter? Any problems?'

And we all turned and yelled at her, 'Shut up!'

Writer-Director Rahul tried to calm us down, 'Now it'll be fine. Trust me. No more panic and listen to Charu.' Then he turned to me, 'Okay curtain!'

I pulled up the curtain and Ashish and Pinky entered the stage. I settled down to prompt and for a while things were going fine. Pinky was acting really well and Ashish seemed to have recovered. The audience was quiet and no one was giggling or even coughing. I could feel my heart stop its mad thudding and begin beating normally again.

Minnie stood next to me in the wings, still swotting her lines as she waited for her cue. Then I heard her take a deep breath and enter the stage and then a ripple of laughter flowed up to me, making me look up.

Minnie was saying her lines with a lot of emotion and expression, dramatically waving her arms—but she was still wearing her glasses and holding the script. She was supposed to be playing Jija Bai, Shivaji's mother!

'Minnie!' I hissed frantically. She turned and frowned at me. I pointed at my nose and mouthed 'glasses' and she looked puzzled, touched her nose, blinked down at the hand holding the script and seemed to wake up to reality. Then right in the middle of Pinky's dialogue she gave the audience a dazzling smile, ducked back into the wings, dropped the glasses and script in my lap and went back on stage again.

That heartbreaking roll of laughter began once more as Rahul started to moan in the corner. Someone in the audience was gasping for breath.

On stage, Minnie gave a glassy smile and said, 'Shivaji, my son...'

Ashish as Shivaji glared at her.

Our friend, the wag in the audience, said helpfully, 'Can you see without your glasses mother Jija Bai? Your son is on the left.'

'Rahul!' I whispered, 'You have to enter now.'

Rahul adjusted his wig and entered as the Bijapur army commander Adil Khan. Things went on so smoothly after that I was more than a bit surprised. And when the scene ended the applause seemed more in relief than praise. The problem was that we still had two more scenes to survive.

The next scene was before the Bijapur army camp. The stage was going to be really crowded because everyone who didn't get a role had been made a soldier. Rahul was pacing around on stage, while behind me in the wings the soldiers were gathering with a lot of clattering of tin swords and nervous whispers.

Rahul yelled, 'Soldiers!' and clumping and thumping, four soldiers played by Ketan, Kaushik, Sudha and Manav entered, wearing turbans, holding spears and swords ... left, right, left, right ... in perfect unison they marched across the stage. And right behind them ... left, right, tail up, trailing his leash, marched Manav's puppy Sooty.

The roar of laughter nearly broke my heart.

'Sooty!' I called desperately, 'Come here, Sooty!'

Minnie, crouching in the opposite wings, whistled, 'Hey Sooty! Come here!'

Sooty stood centre stage, tongue hanging with a stupid doggy grin on his face. He looked at me, then at Minnie, then looked up at Manav who stood guarding the general's tent and seemed to have his eyes closed in prayer. Then he strolled across to the cardboard tree in the corner and began sniffing it. I shut my eyes in horror.

'Manav!' Manav's father suddenly yelled from the audience. 'Take away that dog! Now!'

Manav finally moved, as he dragged Sooty into the wings, left the leash in my hand and marched back on stage thumping his spear.

And oh! You wouldn't believe the laughter! It was like rolling thunder echoing through the puja pandal.

They were acting and shouting away on stage, but think of what I was facing. Have you ever tried to prompt during a play while holding an excited, stage struck puppy with one hand and clutching the script in the other? Sooty was pulling at his leash, dying to go back on stage for the applause.

Prayer was the only solution, 'Oh God, please do something yaar,' I whispered. God wasn't on leave; He'd resigned from the job.

On stage Adil Khan had heard that his son had been killed in battle. Rahul slowly sank down on a chair and said in a shaking voice, 'My son is dead?' then to show grief he was supposed to hit his forehead with his palm but instead he hit his white wig and a cloud of powder rose lazily above him.

'My son!' Rahul quavered as I watched the white powder slowly settle on his nose, 'My ... atchhoo!' Rahul sneezed, 'atchhoo!' and Sooty joined in happily and began to bark.

'Oh you poor thing!' now a female voice. 'Go and blow your nose, Rahul.'

After this the audience decided to join in and take part in the play. It made no difference really. So the dialogues went like this:

Rahul, leading his soldiers, pointing to the north says, 'Be on your guard! There lies the enemy!'

Audience, 'Don't be silly! That's the paan shop.'

Rahul glaring at the audience, 'Shut up!'

Audience, 'Want to fight?'

I was feeling so exhausted I had stopped prompting anyway and Sooty was chewing the script.

Minnie said, 'I give up acting, like forever.'

'You think I'll be a prompter again?'

I don't remember much of the next scene but then to our relief it was the last scene—the fight between Ashish-Shivaji and Rahul-Adil Khan.

Rahul pulled out his sword and yelled, 'Beware, enemy!'

Ashish shouted back, 'This is a fight to the finish!' and reached for his sword. He pulled once, he pulled again and again but it was jammed in the scabbard.

Rahul hopped about the stage, waving his sword in the air. 'Fight, if you are a true warrior, Shivaji!'

Ashish raised a sweaty face. 'Wait, yaar. Can't you see it's stuck?' And as he tugged harder, his turban came off and slid down on to his nose.

Pinky, standing in the corner, had been watching it all with a frown. Suddenly she turned to Rahul and exclaimed, 'Wait, Your Highness!' Then she ran to Ashish and helped him pull out the sword. Then, like an expert costume lady, she carefully adjusted Ashish's turban on his head, moved back a few paces, changed roles to a referee at a boxing match, waved an arm and yelled, 'Come on now! Start fighting!' All she needed was a whistle.

Ashish and Rahul were still fighting when I pulled down the curtain because I couldn't bear it any more.

Ashish marched up to me, still waving his sword and yelled, 'Why'd you do that? I hadn't killed him yet.'

'Shut up!' said Minnie.

'Some fighter,' Pinky muttered angrily, 'You can't even pull out a sword.'

'You even need help with your turban.'

Rahul looked down at Sooty who was now curled up in my lap and said through gritted teeth, 'Where's that idiot Manav? I'm going to kill him!' Sooty looked up with a happy grin and licked my hand.

Then we realized that beyond the curtain, the audience was roaring, 'Come on stage all of you!'

Someone yelled, 'Take a bow!'

We heard the deafening clapping and stared at each other in amazement: were they really applauding? We hauled up the curtain and all of us including Sooty trooped on to the stage and the applause was mind blowing. Would you believe it, we took six bows that evening and someone even garlanded Rahul?

Everyone agreed that it was truly an unforgettable show.

MOHAN, THE MENDICANT AND THE MOO

Adithi Rao

MOHAN sat atop the counter of his father's restaurant and played with the coins inside the cash register. A mendicant wandered up with a brightly decorated bull, and stopped outside the Ganesh Dosa House to peer inside hopefully. The tiny mirrors from the cloth on the animal's back caught the sun and flashed playfully in Mohan's eye.

The child blinked and looked up. He stared. A moo! A moo!

Mohan was friendly with moos. There were two in the cowshed at home, and he was on excellent terms with them. Gauri, the mother, had decided that Mohan was a two-legged calf. And so he enjoyed the same privileges as Gopi, her four-legged one. Gauri licked them clean and fed them milk. She also protected Mohan from the wrath of the household when he stole barfis from the kitchen or dismantled his father's precious, England-made clock to investigate its innards. No one dared raise a hand on Mohan when Gauri was present. Nurtured as he was by this bovine matriarch, it was no wonder that his love extended to the rest of her species as well.

And this is why Mohan dipped a chubby fist into the cash register that day and came up with money. Lots of money! Then he dipped the other one in and caught up the remaining change, cleaning out the tray nicely.

Now all that remained was to get off his perch. This operation gave him pause. With both hands otherwise occupied, he had no way of holding on to any support. Sliding his little round bottom forward until it reached the edge of the counter, he gazed at the ground below. To his adventurous mind, the distance posed no problem at all. It could, of course, have resulted in a broken head. But bah! Mohan wasn't going to let something as trivial as that stop him.

He jumped.

There was a yell of alarm. A tray of water tumblers went flying into the air ... and Mohan landed straight into the arms of Choodamani, the passing waiter! Acting on sheer instinct, Choodamani had flung aside the tray to catch the child in mid-air.

Thanks to the flying tray, Mrs Balambal, wife of the town's most prosperous money lender, got an impromptu bath while gobbling bondas at the nearby table. She gasped and sputtered, dripping like an angry faucet. Luckily for Choodamani, he was too busy rescuing Mohan to notice.

But Nanjuraj, the busboy, came hurrying up, apologizing profusely. Quite without thinking, he grabbed the filthy cloth that he used to clean tables with, and dabbed at Mrs Balambal's sodden bouffant.

'Ayyayyo!' expostulated Balambal, leaping away from the

smelly rag in horror. 'Bloodydonkeymonkeyfellow! You have brains or bubblegum in your head? Just now only I returned from beauty parlour after hair wash and blow dry. Now see what you have done!'

Choodamani, having restored Mohan to the safety of the earth, turned around and began to apologize right and left. In the midst of all the chaos, unnoticed by anyone, Mohan skipped outside and dropped the fistfuls of money into the mendicant's begging bowl. The hundred-rupee notes landed softly into the aluminum vessel. The coins landed with CHANGS! and CLINKS!

Mohan pointed to the bull, indicating that the money was for him. The old mendicant's eyebrows shot up at the sight of so much cash. He glanced furtively into the restaurant. What he saw was a large silk-and-gold bedecked lady sporting an elaborate hairdo making angry swipes at a thin, oily-haired fellow. The fellow was trying to protect his skull without appearing too rude. When at last the edge of her handbag managed to graze his head, she recoiled.

'Cheeeee!' she muttered, glaring accusingly at Nanjuraj as if the oil smears on the shining leather were somehow his fault. Nanjuraj looked up, saw the mess and immediately tried to clean the oil off with his rag.

Only the sudden appearance of Appaji Rao from the kitchen saved Nanju from instant decapitation. Appaji Rao. Father of Mohan, owner of the Ganesh Dosa House. With customary dignity, he gestured for silence. At this, Balambal felt compelled to discontinue her rioting. Poor Nanju heaved a sigh of relief.

However, the old beggar became worried. The proprietor had arrived. Now order would be restored and soon someone would discover the empty cash register. Without a word, the old man turned and slinked away.

Unfortunately, Nandi, his bull, had other plans.

'*Ay, ba. Ba ro! Baaaaa…*' he coaxed with increasing urgency. But the animal refused to budge. The source of Nandi's distraction was the beautiful, wavy-haired boy with big bright eyes. Mohan. The child and the bull gazed at each other fondly. The mendicant dug in his heels, grabbed the bull's rope and leaned backwards with all his might. The bull only tossed his head irritably.

'Pssst … Nandi! Come on, you stupid animal! I'll buy you an extra handful of fresh grass! Just *come*, you son of a cross-eyed goat!'

Mohan frowned. Up until now he had only always heard animals being spoken to with affection. Then, a shout of alarm claimed everyone's attention. All eyes spun around to the cash register, from where the sound had emanated. The mendicant gasped in superstitious fear. There was nobody there. The register had alerted the owner of its own accord!

But then Bangara, the diminutive cook, stepped out from behind the counter, and the mendicant felt weak with relief. At least there was no divine intervention here.

'*Sahib-re! Sahib-re!*' cried Bangara, his eyes wide as saucers. 'All money missing!'

Appaji Rao hurried over to see for himself. At this thrilling juncture, the mendicant thought, 'It's now or never.'

Taking a deep breath, he stepped over the threshold of the Ganesh Dosa House. Bowing low before the proprietor, he pinned an ingratiating smile to his face.

'I was just coming to return the money, *sahib-re*. This little boy (indicating Mohan) gave it to me. He is Lord Krishna incarnate, this son of yours. So generous! So kind to the poor! But you please take it back. No-no, you must, I *insist*! How can a poor man like me digest so much money?' He offered the begging bowl to Appaji Rao.

The restaurant staff grew uncomfortable. Thinking Appaji might strike Mohan, Choodamani sidled up protectively to the child. Appaji Rao gazed down at his son for a long moment. Mohan looked back with frank, clear eyes. Appaji's face softened. Turning to the beggar he said gruffly, 'Keep it.'

'But *sahib-re*!' protested Bangara, scandalized. 'That was one whole day's earnings of the restaurant!'

'Never mind,' said Appaji. 'Once the child has given it, we will not take it back.'

The mendicant left quickly, hardly able to believe his luck. Nandi again proved unwilling to budge. Mohan, who was watching keenly, saw the man aim a swift kick at the animal's hind leg. Reluctantly, Nandi followed his master. Mohan scowled after the mendicant. But moments later, a naughty idea sprang to his over-active brain. His eyes soon began to shine...

When Mohan and his grandfather returned home from the market that day, Mohan was clutching two brightly coloured balloons in his hands. That evening, when the women were busy preparing dinner, Mohan crept to his mother's cupboard and pulled out her wedding sari. It was a splendid silk, decorated with golden peacocks and flower motifs.

In the cow shed, Gauri was peacefully chewing cud, and Gopi was fast asleep. Mohan tied a balloon to each of Gauri's horns and placed the folded sari across her back. She looked at him enquiringly.

'Come, Gauri!' he whispered, looking around to make sure no one was about. Game for anything that her beloved Mohan had set his mind to, Gauri trotted along beside him. Out of the front gate and down the street they went, the balloons bobbing comically above Gauri's head. When they reached the temple square in the market place, Mohan spotted the mendicant and Nandi standing under the peepal tree. Just the ones he was looking for! He led Gauri to a spot close to them. The mendicant was too busy begging to notice him. But Nandi began to pull joyfully on the rope at the sight of his friend.

Holding out his palms, Mohan cried, 'Oh, won't you give a poor old man a few coins?' He called so loudly, over and over again, that people stopped to stare. The beggar glared indignantly at the competition. He felt (rightly so) that he was being made fun of. By now everyone in the vicinity was laughing at the spectacle. It was very funny to watch the little fellow wring his hands in perfect imitation of the old mendicant. More in appreciation for the entertainment than for anything else, they dropped coins into Mohan's palms. But if someone lingered only to stare or enjoy the fun, Gauri butted them till they paid up. Soon the little palms grew so full that the coins had to be transferred into Mohan's pockets. He was stealing the mendicant's business!

Then a regular at the Dosa House spotted Mohan and stared.

'Arrey, isn't that Appaji's son?'

'Impossible!' said his wife.

The man peered into the dusk to get a better look. 'But it is!' he cried. 'What is he doing here?'

'It looks like he's *begging*!' gasped she.

'We'd better take him home. Appaji will have a fit if he finds out about this!'

The couple hurried across to Mohan. Gauri immediately advanced, lowering her head threateningly. The man stepped back hastily.

'Little one,' he said to Mohan. 'Come, let's go home.'

Mohan smiled up at the man. Then he walked across to a farmer sitting a short distance away and bought a small bundle of fresh grass. He placed it before Nandi, stroking the animal lovingly in parting.

Then he walked back home with Gauri, while the couple followed at a safe distance from Gauri's balloon-bedecked horns. With every step Mohan took, the coins jingled in his pockets as if singing a little song.

Back at home, everyone was frantic. Choodamani, Bangara and Nanju had gone in search of Mohan.

'Gauri will take care of him,' said Appaji soothingly to his weeping wife, trying to hide his own panic.

'*Sahib-re?*' called a voice from the door. The family hurried into the hall to see who had come. They saw the couple standing beside Mohan and Gauri in the front yard. Mohan's mother and grandmother ran to Mohan, caught him up in their arms and began to kiss him. But he wriggled out of their embrace, slid down to the ground, and went to his father. Emptying the money from his pockets, he held it out to Appaji Rao.

Appaji looked at his son. He looked at the outstretched little palms, and the money that filled them. He opened his mouth to say something, but closed it again. Abruptly he turned and went into his room. The others exchanged frightened glances. 'He's angry!' they whispered.

Only Mohan knew that his father had gone away because he didn't want anyone to see the tears that had sprung to his eyes.

THE SUBSTITOOTH

Jerry Pinto

'NEW teacher, new teacher,' shouted Darius as he ran into the classroom of VIII B.

'Fry my brains with pepper and salt,' said Chandy. 'Who told you?'

'Swarmy is in the hospital,' shouted Darius, punching the air.

'Oh, tomatoes and brains! Who told you?' asked Chandy again.

'No one had to tell me. He's in my Dad's hospital with acute up-en-dee-titis.'

Mike came out and wrote the correct spelling on the board. A-P-P-E-N-D-I-C-I-T-I-S. A barrage of paper balls hit his back.

'Ignoramuses,' he said and returned to his book.

'All for one?' shouted Chandy as a question

'One for all!' shouted the class back. They had seen *The Three Musketeers* together at Shree Cinema, morning show, Sunday at 11. VIII B, Victoria High School, Mahim, was a united class. They were the terror of their teachers and they knew it. They were world-famous in Mahim for being bad.

Mike put down his book.

'And who is the new teacher?' he asked.

Class VIII B would never admit that their leader was Mike—he stood first, he didn't like sports, he liked to read. But though it was never said, everyone knew that he was. Because he could think up some really evil mischief, like mixed-up names.

In the first week of class, when a new teacher walked in, everyone would have swapped names. So the teacher would ask Mike his name and he would say, 'I'm Chandy.'

The class would laugh loudly.

When Chandy was asked his name, he would say, 'Mike.'

The class would laugh again.

And so it would go on—Vasu would say he was Iqbal, who would say he was Vasu; Darius would say he was Keshto, who would say he was Darius—and each time the class would laugh.

'What's the joke? Have you all gone mad?' the teacher would ask, perplexed.

The class would quieten down.

When the teacher asked Chandy to stand up, Mike would get up. When the teacher asked Iqbal for the capital of Brunei, Vasu would shout, 'Bandar Seri Begawan!'

The class would be in splits. Now the teacher knew something was definitely wrong, but didn't quite know what. This caused a delicious amount of confusion, and the boys loved it. Only Swaminathan (Chemystery and Fizz-sicks) knew the correct names of all the boys, because he had the register.

Mike was also the boy who had invented the 'Softest Punch Challenge'. You went up to a Big Boy, from Class IX or Class X (there was no use trying this with someone your size or someone smaller than you), and you said to him, 'Bet you my punch is softer than your punch.'

This would cause the Big Boy to stare at you and say, 'Of course it is.'

'Prove it,' you would say.

Big Boy: 'You're mad or what?'

You: 'You're scared or what?'

Big Boy: 'I'll *pound* you into the ground.'

You: 'See? See? Bet you can't hit softly. I can hit softly. I can hit so softly a butterfly won't feel it. But you can't.'

Big Boy brings his eyebrows together in a frown.

You wiggle your eyebrows. 'So?'

Big Boy: 'Okay, come here.'

Then he punches you gently.

After that you get to punch him hard, really hard, *full-to hard*, DHADDAAM.

Big Boy: 'Ow, ow, ow!'

You: 'Okay, I lose. You win.'

Then you have to run.

That was why Mike was king. He read books and he stood first but he was King.

***

The door flew open again.

'New teacher, new teacher,' shouted Iqbal, running into the room.

'We know,' shouted the class.

'Substitooth,' said Iqbal.

'Don't make me come out there again,' said Mike wearily. 'Sub-sti-*tute*,' he said slowly.

'That's what I said.'

Mike sighed.

'How do you know, my bheja paratha?' Chandy asked Iqbal.

'Dikkoobai,' said Iqbal. It was the name by which the disrespectful louts of VIII B referred to Ms Lysistrata DaCunha, teacher of English and mother of Lancelot (Class VI A) and Lawrence (Class X C).

'Shutt-up you,' said Vasu. 'Dikkoobai doesn't talk to boys outside class, not even her own boys. We all know. No?'

'*She* didn't tell me. She gave me the compo books and pointed to the staff room with her chin, and when I entered they were saying poor Swami ...'

'He's gone barmy!' Chandy interjected. He had been waiting to say it. For Class VIII B loved a rhyme. They hated poetry in which women sang songs in the Outer Hebrides, but they loved a rhyme.

'Swamy is barmy, Swamy is barmy,' they chanted together.

'So now we have a substitooth,' concluded Iqbal.

'Think she's substicute?' asked Vasu. Everyone knew that Vasu had a girlfriend. He could therefore ask questions like that.

'Substicute? Oh, I wouldn't know,' said a lady's voice at the door. 'What do you think?'

Class VIII B felt a moment of unease. This was not what they were used to. They were used to sending new teachers running back to the teachers' room in tears, only to be told there that nothing was worse than VIII B.

But this one was actually smiling!

Mike recovered first.

'Good *morning*, Miss,' he said.

It was a signal. Each boy would now stand up and say 'Good morning, Miss' with just the right degree of goodmannerliness and communitylivinginess and dutifulboyishness that would make it impossible for her to suspect what was coming. Not for Class VIII B the one-time-greeting. Each individual boy would stand up and greet the new teacher, repeatedly, till her nerves were on edge.

The Substitooth seemed immune to the slow torture. She looked at the greeting boys with such lack of interest and expression that they soon fell silent.

She wandered to the window and looked out. Class VIII B was proud that theirs was one of the classes that overlooked the graveyard.

Then she gave a little scream.

'Ghost!' she said.

The whole class raced to the windows.

'Gone now,' said the Substitooth and went to her seat. 'That was my thirty-second ghost and the first in a tuxedo. Have you boys ever seen a ghost?'

'No, Miss,' said Vasu.

'Then what's the point of having a class that looks over the graveyard?' asked the Substitooth.

Vasu did not know what to say to that and sat down.

Mike felt the situation was getting out of hand.

'Do you want to know our names, Miss?' he asked.

'Oh no, I shall never remember. So I shall give you the names that I like. I shall call you Frooze.'

'Frooze?' asked Mike. 'Why Frooze?'

'And why *not* Frooze?' asked the Substitooth. 'After all, take oxygen. Its name is a mistake. It was thought to make acid and hence it was named oxygen. But we know now ...'

And before they knew it, the class was dipping into the mysteries of Chem. This, it seemed to Mike, was terribly unfair. The Substitooth was not playing by the rules. He waited until she came to a pause and jumped in.

'Miss, what is your name?'

'I will tell you,' she said. 'And you may laugh. You may laugh loudly, like this: HA HAHA HAHAHA!'

Her laugh shook the room.

'My name is Freny Daruwalla.'

The class did not feel like laughing now.

'Daru like alcohol?' asked Vasu.

'Yes, as in davaa-daaru,' said the Substitooth.

'My name is Iqbal,' said Vasu.

'I told you I'd never remember your names on the first day. But I'm sure I'll get them by and by.'

'Bye bye, Miss,' said Mike suddenly.

The class perked up happily.

'Bye-bye, Miss.'

'See you, Miss.'

'So long, Miss.'

'We'll miss you, Miss.'

'Miss us, Miss!'

And then they started all over again.

'Bye-bye, Miss.'

'See you, Miss,'

'So long, Miss.'

'We'll miss you, Miss.'

'Miss us, Miss!'

To their delight Miss Daruwalla began to cry.

'Oh you are so mean to me,' she sobbed. 'You are so mean. My father is ill. He has cancer and he needs an operation and I'm working night and day to save money for him. My mother is blind and she needs an operation and my brother would work day and night to save money for her operation but he can't because he has malaria and cholera and I don't think I'm feeling very well ...'

She staggered across to the door and suddenly collapsed.

'Aaai-chhooo,' said Iqbal.

'Dead?' shouted the class.

'Oh my pulao factory,' said Chandy. 'She's dead.'

Dead, dead, the word thundered in every head. It filled Class VIII B with unholy dread. The Principal, Father Praxidese, would see red. And they would be in jail, drinking water and eating bread.

They got to their feet and inched towards where Miss Daruwalla was lying on the floor in an ungainly heap, legs splayed and head to one side. They gathered around her with Mike fighting his way to the centre.

'Give her air, let her breathe,' he was saying.

'See, we said bye and she died!' said Chandy.

'That's why my mother says, "Don't say bye, say I'm coming back,"' said Vasu.

'Is she properly dead?' asked Darius.

'Yes,' said Chandy, 'see her tongue.'

Indeed, Miss Daruwalla's tongue was sticking out of her mouth.

'Call a doctor,' said Chandy.

'Call the police,' said Vasu.

'Don't call the Princy,' said Mike.

And then Miss Daruwalla screamed, 'Bhoot!' and leapt up from the floor, her arms flailing in the air. Class VIII B, united as always, gave a one-for-all-and-all-for-one shriek of terror and jumped back. Chandy fell over Vasu and Mike was cowering on the floor and someone was calling for his mummy.

Miss Daruwalla began to laugh. This time she laughed like a horse.

'You should have seen your faces,' she said. 'Now go back to your places.'

After a while someone asked, 'Is your mother really blind, Miss?'

She giggled.

'No, she's dead. She died with sodawaterbottle glasses but she wasn't blind.'

'Haw, how can you talk like that?' said Vasu.

'She's my mother, she won't mind. But just to be sure, when she comes to visit me tonight, I'll tell her that I made her blind because Class VIII B was naughty. Then I'll give her your names and send her off, shall I?'

The class laughed delightedly.

'Does your father really have cancer, Miss?'

'No, he's dead,' said Miss Daruwalla briefly. 'He was in the army. Do you know what he left me in his will?'

'No, Miss, what?'

'He left me his service revolver. Every month I take it out and clean it and oil it and put it back. Now the best-behaved boy will get to come home and help me do that. How's that?'

***

No one knew how she managed it but Miss Daruwalla had Class VIII B eating out of her hand. And she showed them forty ghosts before the year was up.

MISCHIEVOUS
ANIMALS

FRIENDS OR ENEMIES?

Kavitha Mandana

RAMBO came to our house full grown and readymade. Tina Aunty had already house trained him years ago. Every time I had stopped by at Vidyut's house on the way home from school, Rambo would come running out to welcome us. He was adorably fat. Just wagging his tail made him tired—because that meant shifting his huge bottom (which was attached to his always-happy tail) from side to side, very fast. So though Tina Aunty's chocolate cake was world-famous, Rambo was the real reason we all went to Vidyut's house so often.

One day, Tina Aunty came home looking glum and told Mama, 'You know, Situ, we're moving to Dubai.' My first thought was not, 'Oh no! Now I'll miss having Vidyut around.' Instead I wondered, 'Will they take Rambo with them?'

Answering my prayers, Tina Aunty continued, 'Yes, I know Meenu, it is a promotion for Vikram, and we will have a great future there … but what about Rambo?'

I won't tell you about all the promises I made to Mama about taking care of Rambo. But within two weeks, Rambo had moved in with us. And once Papa realized that Rambo politely did his potty business somewhere at the back of the garden, even he relaxed and allowed himself to fall in love with Rambo. Now and then he'd say, 'Just remember that this Rambo fellow is not a guard dog, okay.' That was true ... Rambo wagged his big bottom happily at whoever came to the gate.

But not everyone welcomed Rambo at first. Pullu, our cat, was quite irritated at his arrival. And she played all her mischievous tricks on him.

One day, just a few days after he'd arrived, I ran out when I heard some wild barking and angry screaming. There, where the maid had just hung out the week's clean bedsheets to dry, Rambo was scrambling about, leaping on the sheets with his dirty paws. He was acting totally crazy. The maid was furious, one bedsheet was ripped down the middle. The big tamasha of Rambo attacking the sheets only came to an end when the clothesline snapped and all the sheets collapsed over Rambo, smothering him for a moment.

Later, as Mama put all the Rambo-footprint sheets back in the washing machine, she grumbled, 'I hope we haven't made a mistake by adopting Rambo.' I kept quiet. Because only I had seen Pullu sneak away from between the rows of clean sheets, with Rambo's bone in her mouth.

After that, I started spying on the two of them. It was like a TV show. *Rambo and Pullu* or *Friends and Enemies.* One day, from upstairs I spotted Rambo fast asleep, snoring loudly. Pullu sneaked up. She quietly picked up the bone next to Rambo's snout, turned delicately on her four paws and tiptoed away. Her nostrils flared with anticipation at all the meat still left on the bone. Her whiskers twitched with happiness and she almost leapt onto the window ledge to make her escape, when she stopped.

To me it seemed like she realized that stealing a bone from Rambo would be no fun if he didn't know that it was *she*, Pullu, who'd taken it. So, she turned around, and gave the fat sleeping Labrador a sharp prod on his big bottom. Only when he jerked awake with a start did she leap out of his reach, up the neem tree—tauntingly holding up the meat-filled bone. A still half-asleep Rambo barked furiously at being woken up from a happy dream probably featuring lots of people cuddling him. AND discovering that his precious bone was gone. He clumsily circled the neem tree, trying to look menacing.

After some hectic barking, Rambo lost interest and loped off on hearing the horn of the garbage truck. Though Pullu could now enjoy the bone in peace, once Rambo had vanished, it somehow didn't taste as good. Listlessly, she polished the bone clean, stretched and then set to clean herself before dozing off.

Sometimes when she was bored, Pullu jumped onto Rambo's back from the tree above him, almost giving him a heart attack. Then she'd run off, just staying out of his reach, as he panted after her. Soon, everyone realized that all the noise and barking was just Pullu being a naughty cat, NOT Rambo being a bad dog.

But somewhere along all this chasing, bone-stealing and angry barking, they became friends.

Pullu never let anyone carry her or cuddle her. But once, when Rambo was sick and weak with a bad stomach, I tiptoed downstairs at night to check on him. And instead of a weak and dying dog, I found a happily snoring one, with Pullu curled up against his fat stomach.

One day, it was Pullu's turn to be jolted out of her sleep by the shrill sound of screeching brakes. Mama always said that Pullu's instincts are very sharp. She noticed that Pullu was instantly alert and seemed to feel something was seriously wrong. Pullu looked down and realized that Rambo wasn't around. She dashed off, almost like she knew he was in danger.

Mama caught the sense of panic from Pullu and yelled out for me to see what had happened. I looked out from upstairs and saw Pullu streak across the garden and onto the road. She raced down the pavement to the intersection and there she froze. There was a large crowd. She slowed down and Rani Aunty later told us she spotted Pullu making her way gingerly between a hundred pairs of legs. There at the centre of the crowd, lay a smashed motorbike, a dazed rider and an unconscious Rambo. There was no time to lose. Pullu raced back to the house.

In seconds, she was on the kitchen counter, mewing pitifully at Mama. When Mama responded with a piece of fish, Pullu swept it away impatiently. THAT got Mama's attention—something had to be wrong for Pullu to refuse fish. Mama hitched up her sari and followed the cat out of the back door. Within seconds, Pullu and Mama had joined me in racing down the road towards the crowd of people.

When we arrived, we saw that the rider of the bike hadn't been injured, so all the crowd's attention and sympathy was on the 'poor dog'. Rambo still lay on his side, looking dazed but no longer unconscious. THAT was a relief. While people stroked and clucked over him, he caught Pullu's eye and gave her a weak tail-wag. The bike was a wreck, so it was only luck that had saved Rambo … and maybe his fat bottom, which wasn't easy to run over!

Crowds are no place for a cat, so with Rambo safe, Pullu slunk away. Later, after the crowd had dispersed, only Rani Aunty stayed back telling us about how Pullu had behaved. We then walked Rambo home, slowly.

As we approached our gate, we heard loud, angry barking. That was Duke, the fatter and lazier Alsatian from next door. Just as I began to wonder what the problem could be, I spotted Pullu. She'd leaped onto our wall from the roof of Duke's kennel. In her mouth she had a big bone of mutton, dripping with gravy. As she jumped down into our garden, we heard poor Duke's barks get more frenzied.

Pullu padded along ahead of us and dropped her trophy beside Rambo's water bowl. And tired as he was, Rambo plonked himself down beside this new bone, licking up the gravy happily.

I'd never seen Pullu look so motherly! I also knew that from now, she and Rambo were friends forever. Her mischief would be only reserved for poor Duke.

MISHTI PLAYS WITH FIRE

Gillian Wright

MISHTI loved digging. Sitting in muddy puddles satisfied her, and digging in mud delighted her. And so she, and sometimes Soni too, were often more black than golden. But they were never allowed into the house as black Labradors and always had to have a bucket bath first, and be rubbed with a towel while they played towel tug-of-war.

During the winter it's cold in Delhi, and so they were kept away from mud and baths as much as possible as they could easily catch a chill. But one winter day, they had a muddy morning and so Gilly had to wash them. She rinsed the shampoo out of their fur and rubbed them as dry as she could.

In the New Delhi dog parlours Gilly had seen people use hair dryers to dry dogs after a bath. But Gilly knew that Soni and Mishti didn't like them. In fact, they behaved as if hair dryers were evil aliens from outer space. When she pointed her hair dryer at them, they would bare their teeth and bark dementedly. Strangely enough, they had the same reaction to toothbrushes. If you held out a toothbrush and walked towards them they would bark hysterically and reverse out of the room. They didn't like the vacuum cleaner either.

So as Gilly wanted Soni and Mishti to dry off quickly after their bath, and a hair dryer was out of the question, she turned on the fan heater in the bedroom, shut the door to keep the warmth inside and went about her work. She thought they would settle down in their dog-beds in front of the heater and soon get dry.

It was a busy sort of day. Gilly started working on her laptop in their office room. Two carpenters were in the house making some more bookshelves, as the one thing Mark and Gilly had a lot of was books. Every day more arrived in the post. Piles of them lay around the house. It was a busy day upstairs too. There was an advertising office there and they had lots of visitors of their own.

About ten minutes after Gilly started work, Bubbly came in, panic-stricken.

'Bedroom *ke darvaze ke niche se dhuan nikal rahi hai!*' she cried.

Gilly ran across the sitting room to the bedroom. Smoke was indeed drifting out from underneath the door. Inside the dogs were barking. She threw the door open.

A terrifying sight met her eyes! The room was ablaze, flames leaping up the curtains. It was full of smoke. Her first priority was the dogs. She called, 'Mishti, Soni, come!' They trotted out immediately and once she saw they were safe, she shut them in the spare bedroom a good way away from the fire. Meanwhile Kaka had heard the noise. He immediately rushed to the Master

Switch to turn off the electricity supply to the house. Gilly and Bubbly hurried to fill buckets with water. The carpenters came to help and, seeing the smoke, the office staff from upstairs ran downstairs with buckets. In just a few minutes there was a swift supply of buckets and pots of water pouring on to the flames. Soon the fire was extinguished.

At this point, Mark, who had been reading a very interesting and absorbing book in the garden, and so hadn't heard a thing, walked in, and asked, 'Has anything happened?'

Gilly and Bubbly looked at each other in amazement. Black smoke still swirled around the sitting room. The bedroom curtains and blinds and some books and papers were destroyed and the ceiling and walls were black.

Everyone now had time to think. How could this have happened?

Gilly went to let the dogs out of the spare bedroom. She looked at both of them. Soni was very happy to be let out and ran around licking everyone within reach, a big smile on her face and her big, floppy ears set forward. Mishti's eyes were sparkling with mischief. Mother and daughter were the only witnesses to the incident, and they weren't talking.

So Gilly went back to the scene of the crime and tried to piece the evidence together like a detective. There were plenty of clues. On the floor the fan heater looked like a painting by the artist Salvador Dali. Its plastic casing had melted into a bizarre, omelette-like shape. Around it were the noxious black remains of a dog-bed.

A light bulb turned on in Gilly's brain. She suddenly realized what must have happened.

Mishti was a playful dog. She played wrestling with her friends in the park, she played wrestling with her puppies, and she played wrestling with her round, cozy, foam dog-bed from the local pet-shop. Unlike the others, it couldn't wrestle back, so she could easily throw it around the room. After her morning walk she would, on a normal day, have a nap. However, the excitement of a muddy morning and a winter bath must have given her extra bounce. Gilly visualized Mishti, a slightly manic look in her eyes, playing with the dog-bed until she tossed it on top of the fan heater. In only a minute or so the dog-bed must have caught fire, and after that the curtains.

There were lessons to be learned here. No more fan heaters anywhere near Mishti, and no more flammable dog-beds from the pet shop.

They had been so lucky that there were so many helpful people around. So lucky.

For the next week or so Gilly and Mark and the dogs slept in the spare bedroom. The painters moved into their bedroom, with all their paraphernalia. They kept on complaining about the number of coats of paint they needed to cover up the blackened ceiling and walls.

Mishti was a unique dog, thought Gilly. Some dogs saved their owners from danger, but Mishti had nearly burned the house down.

TRAVELLING WITH GRANDFATHER'S ZOO

Ruskin Bond

'ALL aboard!' shrieked Popeye, Grandmother's pet parrot, as the family climbed aboard the Lucknow Express. We were moving for some months from Dehra to Lucknow, and as Grandmother had insisted on taking her parrot along, Grandfather and I insisted on bringing our pets too—a teenaged tiger (Grandfather's) and a small squirrel (mine). But we thought it prudent to leave the python behind.

In those days trains in India were not so crowded and it was possible to travel with a variety of creatures. Grandfather had decided to do things in style by travelling first-class, so we had a four-berth compartment of our own, and Timothy, the tiger, had an entire berth to himself. Later, everyone agreed that Timothy behaved perfectly throughout the journey. Even the guard admitted that he could not have asked for a better passenger: no stealing from vendors, no shouting at coolies, no breaking of railway property, no spitting on the platform.

All the same, the journey was not without incident and before we reached Lucknow, there was excitement enough for everyone.

To begin with, Popeye objected to vendors and other people poking their hands in through the windows. Before the train had moved out of Dehra station, he had nipped two fingers and tweaked a ticket-inspector's ear.

No sooner had the train started moving than Chips, my squirrel, emerged from my pocket to examine his surroundings. Before I could stop him, he was out of the compartment door, scurrying along the corridor.

Chips discovered that the train was a squirrel's paradise, almost all the passengers having bought large quantities of roasted peanuts before the train pulled out. He had no difficulty in making friends with both children and grown-ups, and it was an hour before he returned to our compartment, his tummy almost bursting.

'I think I'll go to sleep,' said Grandmother, covering herself with a blanket and stretching out on the berth opposite Timothy's. 'It's been a tiring day.'

'Aren't you going to eat anything?' asked Grandfather.

'I'm not hungry—I had some soup before we left. You two help yourselves from the tiffin basket.'

Grandmother dozed off, and even Popeye started nodding, lulled to sleep by the clackety-clack of the wheels and the steady puffing of the steam engine.

'Well, I'm hungry,' I said. 'What did Granny make for us?'

'Ham sandwiches, boiled eggs, a roast chicken, gooseberry pie. It's all in the tiffin basket under your berth.'

I tugged at the large basket and dragged it into the centre of the compartment. The straps were loosely tied. No sooner had I undone them than the lid flew open, and I let out a gasp of surprise.

In the basket was Grandfather's pet python, curled up contentedly on the remains of our dinner. Grandmother had insisted that we leave the python behind, and Grandfather had let it loose in the garden. Somehow, it had managed to smuggle itself into the tiffin basket.

'Well, what are you staring at?' asked Grandfather from his corner.

'It's the python,' I said. 'And it has finished all our dinner.'

Grandfather joined me, and together we looked down at what remained of the food. Pythons don't chew, they swallow: outlined along the length of the large snake's sleek body were the distinctive shapes of a chicken, a pie and six boiled eggs. We couldn't make out the ham sandwiches, but presumably these had been eaten too because there was no sign of them in the basket. Only a few apples remained. Evidently, the python did not care for apples.

Grandfather snapped the basket shut and pushed it back beneath the berth.

'We mustn't let Grandmother see him,' he said. 'She might think we brought him along on purpose.'

'Well, I'm hungry,' I complained. Just then, Chips returned from one of his forays and presented me with a peanut.

'Thanks,' I said. 'If you keep bringing me peanuts all night, I might last until morning.'

But it was not long before I felt sleepy. Grandfather had begun to nod and the only one who was wide awake was the squirrel, still intent on investigating distant compartments.

A little after midnight there was a great clamour at the end of the corridor. Grandfather and I woke up. Timothy growled in his sleep, and Popeye made complaining noises.

Suddenly there were cries of 'Saap, saap!' (Snake, snake!)

Grandfather was on his feet in a moment. He looked under the berth. The tiffin basket was empty.

'The python's out,' he said, and dashed out of our compartment in his pyjamas. I was close behind.

About a dozen passengers were bunched together outside the washroom door.

'Anything wrong?' asked Grandfather casually.

'We can't get into the toilet,' said someone. 'There's a huge snake inside.'

'Let me take a look,' said Grandfather. 'I know all about snakes.'

The passengers made way for him, and he entered the washroom to find the python curled up in the washbasin. After its heavy meal it had become thirsty and, finding the lid of the tiffin basket easy to pry up, had set out in search of water.

Grandfather gathered up the sleepy, overfed python and stepped out of the washroom. The passengers hastily made way for them.

'Nothing to worry about,' said Grandfather cheerfully. 'It's just a harmless young python. He's had his dinner already, so no one is in any danger!' And he marched back to our compartment with the python in his arms. As soon as I was inside, he bolted the door.

Grandmother was sitting up on her berth.

'I knew you'd do something foolish behind my back,' she scolded. 'You told me you'd got rid of that creature, and all the time you've been hiding it from me.'

Grandfather tried to explain that we had nothing to do with it, that the python had smuggled itself into the tiffin basket, but Grandmother was unconvinced. 'What will Mabel do when she sees it!' she cried despairingly.

My Aunt Mabel was a schoolteacher in Lucknow. She was going to share our new house, and she was terrified of all reptiles, particularly snakes.

'We won't let her see it,' said Grandfather. 'Back it goes into the tiffin basket.'

Early next morning, the train steamed into Lucknow. Aunt Mabel was on the platform to receive us.

Grandfather let all the other passengers get off before he emerged from the compartment with Timothy on a chain. I had Chips in my pocket, suitcase in both hands. Popeye stayed perched on Grandmother's shoulder, eyeing the busy platform with considerable distrust.

Aunt Mabel, a lover of good food, immediately spotted the tiffin basket, picked it up and said, 'It's not very heavy. I'll carry it out to the taxi. I hope you've kept something for me.'

'A whole chicken,' I said.

'We hardly ate anything,' said Grandfather.

'It's all yours, Aunty!' I added.

'Oh, good!' exclaimed Aunt Mabel. 'It's been ages since I

tasted something cooked by your grandmother.' And after that there was no getting the basket away from her.

Glancing at it, I thought I saw the lid bulging, but Grandfather had tied it down quite firmly this time and there was little likelihood of its suddenly bursting open.

An enormous 1950 Chevrolet taxi was waiting outside the station, and the family tumbled into it. Timothy got onto the back seat, leaving enough room for Grandfather and me. Aunt Mabel sat in front with Grandmother, the tiffin basket on her lap.

'Tell the taxi driver where to take us, dear,' said Grandmother. 'He's looking rather nervous.'

Aunt Mabel gave instructions to the driver and the taxi shot off in a cloud of dust.

'Well, here we go!' said Grandfather. 'I'm looking forward to settling into the new house.'

Popeye, perched proudly on Grandmother's shoulder, kept one suspicious eye on the quivering tiffin basket.

'All aboard!' he squawked. 'All aboard!'

When we got to our new house, we found a light breakfast waiting for us on the dining table.

'It isn't much,' said Aunt Mabel. 'But we'll supplement it with the contents of your hamper.' And placing the basket on the table, she removed the lid.

The python was half-asleep, with an apple in its mouth. Aunt Mabel was no Eve, to be tempted. She fainted away.

Grandfather promptly picked up the python, took it into the garden, and draped it over a branch of a guava tree.

When Aunt Mabel recovered, she insisted that there was

a huge snake in the tiffin basket. We showed her the empty basket.

'You're seeing things,' said Grandfather.

'It must be the heat,' I said.

Grandmother said nothing. But Popeye broke into shrieks of maniacal laughter, and soon everyone, including a slightly hysterical Aunt Mabel, was doubled up with laughter.

BRINGING UP MOMEE

Vandana Bist

MOMEE firmly believes—or believed till that day—that I, her only offspring, wasn't human. She said I was more a curious tropical creature. Okay, so I am a little slow at times, like chewing each bite thirty-two times, sometimes even sixty-four. Or taking a day or two to finish my breakfast.

Momee says I really get her goat, but I'm only a little kid… (puns are fun!)

That Sunday Momee was at her eruptive, volcanic, and metaphoric best, or worst.

And I maintain—till date—that what happened wasn't my fault.

THAT DAY MOMMEE
OVERDID THE 'SLOTH' BIT.
THE HALF MOON LOOKED
SULKY, OR WAS IT THAT
FREAKY BOOK I HAD BEEN
READING?

MOMMEEE!!
SLOTHY'S HUNGRY! SLOTHY WANTS FOOOOD!!!
A BUNCH OF CECROPIA LEAVES, PLEASE!
AND A BIG BOWL OF RED, JUICY ANTS... YUMMM!
OH! OKAY! I'LL FIX MY DINNER. GOOD NIGHT MOMMEEE!!
SO, WHO CALLED HER A SLOTH?
NO NO NO!! NO NO! NO! NO! NOOOOOO
WHAAAT WAS THAAAT?!?
MY LITTLE GIRL... A SLOTH!!
MY LITTLE LAZY BONES... NO! NO! MY LITTLE GIRL... FAST ASLEEP! WHEW!!! IT WAS A NIGHTMARE AFTER ALL!!
I SHOULD NEVER HAVE CALLED HER A SLOTH! I HOPE IT WAS A NIGHTMARE !!!!

SLOW EATERS ARE SMART EATERS!!
AND THEN ONWARDS.....
DIRT MAKES KIDS HAPPIER HEALTHIER SMARTER!
BOOKS! BOOKS! BOOKS! SHE WILL BE A WRITER SOMEDAY!
THAT BOOK WAS ONE GOOD READ!!!
MY PRINCESS..... CROWNED IN HER MESSY CURLS!
SIGHHH!!!
UGHHH!! FAKE FUNGII
MISS LOTHY!!!
VAMPIRE BOOKS
SHAPE SHIFTING AND WORD POWER
A.K. REELING
SHE SOUNDS LIKE A BOOK OF QUOTES!
I WAS A BUTTERFLY ONCE!!

MISCHIEF-MAKING
FLOATING
GHOSTS

JIMMY THE JINN

Ruskin Bond

JIMMY was (and presumably still is) a jinn. Now a jinn isn't really a human like us. A jinn is a spirit creature from another world who has assumed, for a lifetime, the physical aspect of a human being. Jimmy was a true jinn and he had the jinn's gift of being able to elongate his arm at will.

It was during the half-term examinations that I stumbled on Jimmy's secret. We had been set a particularly difficult algebra paper but I had managed to cover a couple of sheets with correct answers and was about to forge ahead on another sheet when I noticed someone's hand on my desk. At first I thought it was the invigilator's. But when I looked up there was no one beside me.

Could it be the boy sitting directly behind? No, he was engrossed in his question paper and had his hands to himself. Meanwhile, the hand on my desk had grasped my answer sheets and was cautiously moving off. Following its descent, I found that it was attached to an arm of amazing length and pliability. This moved stealthily down the desk and slithered across the floor, shrinking all the while, until it was restored to its normal length. Its owner was of course one who had never been any good at algebra.

I had to write out my answers a second time but after the exam I went straight up to Jimmy, told him I didn't like his game and threatened to expose him. He begged me not to let anyone know, assured me that he couldn't really help himself, and offered to be of service to me whenever I wished. It was tempting to have Jimmy as my friend, for with his long reach he would obviously be useful. I agreed to overlook the matter of the pilfered papers and we became the best of pals.

THE LONG AND SHORT OF IT

Bijal Vachharajani

RASHMI was the youngest in her family. Which was why she was also the shortest. Most nights, before drifting off to sleep, she would line up her family in her head. First she would make Mummy stand, because she was tallest at five feet seven inches and one point five centimetres. Then Papa, who had just missed being the tallest person in the house by one point five centimetres. Next came Chaitu didi, who was also taller than her. In fact, Rashmi was sure that if they had a dog, she'd also be taller than her.

It really was not fair. What was also not fair was that Rashmi's family had just moved to Mumbai where the buildings towered over her. They were way taller than the houses in Delhi.

Much to Rashmi's dismay, her friends in their building society were also taller. There was Tanaz who laughed so much that her freckled face looking like a flaming red cricket ball. Then there was Cyrus, who refused to be separated from his bicycle. He'd say something and then 'tring tring' ring the cycle's bell. It would have been rather annoying, but Cyrus was the oldest of them all. So, they hung on to his every word. Every Single Word. Followed by Every Single Tring. And lastly, there was Nishita, who was younger than Rashmi, but guess what? She was also taller than her.

Every day after school, Rashmi and Didi would change out of their grey-and-white uniforms and swap them for a T-shirt and pair of shorts, gulp down chocolate milk and a snack, and run down to play with their friends. Together, they'd pretend to be as cool as Julian, Dick, George, Anne and Timothy of the Famous Five. Rashmi of course was the dog, because as Cyrus laughed and said, she was always following them around like a happy puppy. 'If she had a tail, she'd wag it,' he laughed, tring-tringing the cycle bell. Everyone laughed, even Rashmi, though her face fell slightly. Everyone always teased her about being the smallest and the shortest.

They explored the abandoned ground behind their society, climbing over the cement and stone rubble, pretending it was the ruins of a castle. They even fashioned a flag out of an old saree, but the next day someone took it. The five of them would go for long picnics on their terrace, except for when it was raining, because then big fat raindrops fell on their butter-chutney sandwiches, making them soggy.

Now it was Diwali vacation and everyone was Bored. Tanaz was supposed to go meet her grandparents in Udwada while Rashmi and Didi were to go back to Delhi. But then suddenly there had been some unexpected rainfall in Mumbai, and now they were stuck in the city. Whoever heard of rain in October? And that too rain that flooded Mr Batliwala's house; that filled up the streets and crept up to their knees, and everyone laughed because it crept up until Rashmi's shoulders.

But now the waters had receded and everyone was home, and very Bored.

'I am bored,' said Tanaz.

'B.O.R.E.D,' nodded Didi.

'With a capital B,' said Nishita.

'Tring, tring,' replied Cyrus.

'I know what we can do!' Cyrus was so excited he kept ringing his cycle's bell until everyone begged him to stop. 'We will play planchette.'

'What's that?' Rashmi asked, crinkling her nose at the thought of walking down a plank, pirate style.

'YES!' Nishita yelled, and then dropped her voice to a whisper. 'Of course, you're too small to know what it is, Rashmi.'

'For the 678th time, I am older than you,' Rashmi huffed, crossing her arms and straightening her back angrily. 'By 15 months and six days.'

'Well, then how come you don't know what planchette is,' Tanaz laughed. 'It's a game to call spirits! Everybody knows that. Come on, let's go down to my place.'

The five of them raced down to Tanaz's house. Rashmi's heart started beating wildly, louder than their footsteps. Calling spirits? That sounded dangerous. How could it be a game? What did that even mean? What if they called a mean, angry one who wanted revenge on the person who stole their pencils right before the exam? Or what if they called Naani and then she would want to know why Rashmi had dropped chocolate milk on her photo and pretended that it was pigeon snot?

The five of them clattered into Tanaz's room and locked it from inside. Her mother was at work, so there was no one to interrupt them.

'So here's how it works,' said Cyrus and paused. He looked bereft as he couldn't ring his cycle bell. Delnaz Aunty did not allow muddy bikes into her house. He pulled out a white chart paper and drew several squares around its borders and scrawled alphabets and numbers on it with an orange sketch pen. In the centre of the chart, he drew a wobbly circle.

'We need a coin,' said Didi.

Everyone turned out their pockets. No coins there. Nishita had a ten-rupee note, but Cyrus deemed it most unhelpful. Instead, they sneaked into Tanaz's mother's room and twisted the cap off her Pond's talcum powder.

They placed it carefully atop the circle, a pink blob on the white paper. 'All right,' said Nishita, 'Everyone put their finger on the cap.'

'Ahem,' Cyrus frowned at her. 'It's my game, I will tell everyone what to do, Nishita.' Nishita scowled and tossed her hair back. 'Well,' he continued, 'place your fingers on the cap.'

'That's what I said,' Nishita said with a loud HMPH. Cyrus ignored her. Rashmi put a trembling index finger on the cap. There was barely any space on the cap now.

'OOooooOOOO Spirit! We implore you to visit us. OOooooOOOO Spirit! Is anyone there?' Cyrus chanted like the priest in the temple. Nishita and Didi closed their eyes solemnly, while Rashmi squinted through one eye. Tanaz collapsed into giggles, her face as pink as the talcum powder cap. 'Shut up,' hissed Didi. 'You will anger the spirits. And then they will haunt you forever.' That got Tanaz quiet. All everyone could hear was Cyrus chanting 'OOoooooOOOO Spirit! Are you here?'

Rashmi's left toe was feeling ticklish but she was too scared to move a muscle. Just as she couldn't bear it any more, the cap began to move! It moved slowly—first to the letter Y, then E, and then all the way to the other side to S. 'YES!' Nishita yelled and everyone shushed her.

'Welcome OOoooOOO Spirit,' said Cyrus, sounding like he was talking from the back of an old cave. 'Will you tell us your name?'

The cap moved. N... O...! Beads of sweat were trickling down Cyrus's brow.

'Ummm okay, OOoooooOOOO Spirit,' he said. 'Can you tell us how you died?'

Y... E ... S ...

I ... W... A ... S ... K ... I ... L ... L ... E ... D

Rashmi opened her eyes again because Didi whimpered a soft 'Oh no...' Cyrus was looking like he wanted to be sick and Tanaz and Nishita were holding on to each other.

'OOoooooOOOO Spirit,' Cyrus managed to stammer out the words. 'Why were you killed?'

B ... E ... C ... A ... U ... S ... E ... I ... W ... O ... U ... L ... D ... N ... T ... S ...T... O ... P...

'Stop what?' Tanaz whispered. 'I think *we* should stop.'

'Shut up,' Didi said. 'We need to know what ... stop what ... perhaps we can help. Cyrus, Cyrus, ask.'

'OOoooooOOOO Spirit,' Cyrus said very slowly. 'Who ... who...?'

M ...Y ... F ... R ... I ... E ... N ... D ...

The cap was moving non-stop now, sliding from one side of the chart to the other, as if it couldn't stop, wouldn't stop, until it had its say.

'Nooo, noooo,' Rashmi whispered. 'Stop this guys, I am scared.' She grabbed Cyrus's arm, but he shook it off. 'Stop being a baby,' he hissed at her. 'Don't remove your finger from the cap, whatever you do. OOooooooOOOO Spirit, why did your friend...'

I ... C ... A ... L ... L ... E ... D ... H ... E ... R ... S ... H ... O ... R ... T

Just then the window in Tanaz's room opened with a loud bang. A gust of wind tore a plastic bag and tossed it into the air. The blue bag hovered above the chart for a few seconds, gleaming, and then slowly drifted on top of Nishita's head. It all happened in a matter of seconds.

Everyone began screaming. Cyrus leapt up and ran out of the room, his hands flailing above his head, as if he was trying to ward off a flock of mosquitoes. Tanaz ran after him clutching Nishita's hand and dragging her along. Didi was curled up into a ball, whispering 'No ... No, please ... no.' Rashmi sat on the floor, her shoulders shaking.

Didi looked up as Cyrus, Tanaz, and Nishita crept back into the room.

'Rashmi!' Nishita said a little weakly, leaning on the wall for support. 'That wasn't funny.'

'Not funny at all,' said Tanaz, her face now pinker than the talcum powder cap.

Rashmi couldn't answer, she was too busy laughing.

THE SPOOK

Bulbul Sharma

AS soon as Bubo woke up he made a mental list of all the mischievous things he could do that day. Not that Bubo really slept at night since ghosts hardly ever need to sleep unless they are recharging their batteries. He just hung himself upside down on a tree in the garden and watched the clouds as they sailed over the moon.

Bubo was transparent but had a faint glow that kept changing according to his moods and this ghostly form was lit by a single-cell battery. The battery also helped when he needed to change into something or someone totally different, which happened quite often. It was such fun to suddenly become a new thing—new face, new voice and new hands and feet. Sometimes Bubo became a strange animal or bird with features that no one had ever seen before. His parents, also spooks, much larger and brighter than him, often scolded him for changing his form so often and running his battery down but he just could not stop himself.

So on this bright, sunny morning he jumped down from the tree, wiped his face with a dew-drenched leaf, and floated out into the garden. First on his naughty things-to-do list was to play a trick on the cat. She was an enormous, evil-eyed cat. Bubo did not like her because she had once attacked his pet, a talking myna. Now the myna refused to talk anymore.

Bubo adjusted his digital watch, put the timer on and changed himself into a huge bumblebee with an antenna that buzzed. Then he jumped and landed right on the cat's nose.

Fifteen seconds. Twenty-nine feet. A record. The cat leapt up with a screech so loud that it made all the leaves on the tree shiver. She put her paw out to shake the bee off but the bee now turned into a chocolate biscuit. The cat licked her lips and tried to eat it but it became a bee again and she quickly spat it out.

Bubo laughed and clapped his hands. Of course there was no sound, as you may have guessed, but the cat sensed that Bubo was hovering nearby and fled under the table.

Next on Bubo's list to tease was the irritating rat who kept chewing up everyone's slippers. Bubo made himself into a juicy, ripe mango and rolled down to the kitchen. The rat lived in the dustbin outside the kitchen. As soon as he saw the mango he scampered across to grab it. Bubo-the-mango now rolled under the table. The rat tried to crawl under the table but before he could do it, Bubo swiftly changed himself into a radio and began to blare loud rock music. The rat jumped up in fright and landed on Bubo who had now turned himself into a long, snake-like slipper and hissed into the rat's ears. The rat ran as fast as he could back to the dustbin and decided never to touch any slippers again.

Bubo, very pleased with himself, stretched out his wavy arms and did a few cartwheels on the floor. Tomorrow he would get a gooey cake for the cat and a juicy mango for the rat for letting him play these pranks on them.

Bubo decided to go out into the garden again. The birds could see him and always chirped cheerfully to say 'hello'. But today they were looking very sad. A boy had hit one of them with his slingshot and the injured bird now hid in one corner, nursing its broken wing.

This nasty boy loved teasing birds, throwing stones at them when they came out to eat the seeds his mother scattered every morning for them. Bubo decided that it was time to teach him a lesson. It was fun to be naughty but being cruel to other creatures was not good.

Not good at all.

So he folded himself into a shiny, red ball and rolled on the grass. The boy saw him and shouted with glee. He quickly picked up Bubo-the-ball and tossed him up. Bubo bounced back on the boy's nose. This time the boy threw him higher in the air and guess what happened? Bubo changed into a giant bird. He clasped his huge claws around the boy's neck and took him right up into the clouds. The boy screamed in terror. The cat safe inside the house heard him, the rat snug in the dustbin heard him, the birds the boy had thrown stones at heard him and his mother thought she heard him but then decided it was the cat mewing next door.

Bubo floated over the clouds and landed on top of a

mountain, still clutching the boy in his claws. Then he set him down on the grass. The boy, a bit dazed, sat there scratching his nose. He could not understand what was happening to him. He was not hurt but his head was spinning like mad. Then he saw the giant bird swoop down again, its claws stretched out like a fan. The boy opened his mouth to scream but the bird put one, long claw out and tickled the boy's nose. The boy did not know whether to laugh or cry. The bird stared at him, its large yellow eyes gleaming like fire. Then he lifted a huge stone. The boy quickly moved back. He thought the stone was going to land on his head. But Bubo-the-bird threw the stone up in the air. It burst open and a hundred tiny red, blue and green birds flew out. They came and sat on the boy's head, his arms and a dozen sat on his stomach to tickle him. Suddenly the boy could understand what they were saying. 'Please don't throw stones at us. We have never harmed you so why should you harm us?' they chirruped, flying around his head.

'I won't. I am sorry,' said the boy and the birds vanished. Suddenly, the huge shiny ball appeared again and a long rubbery arm picked him up.

Bubo tossed the boy high up in the air and caught him again. 'You won't throw stones at the birds again, will you? Promise?' he asked in a squeaky voice. The boy shouted back, 'I promise. I will never harm them.' He was no longer scared and was having a great time as Bubo-the-ball played catch with him. Then they flew over the ocean and saw a whale. Bubo took him through the clouds and he saw a golden eagle. The shiny red ball flew him all over the city, over his house and he saw his mother in the garden feeding the birds. Then they came home and the wonderful red ball just vanished.

Next morning, Bubo, invisible once more, since his battery needed to be charged, sat on the tree and talked to the birds. The cat was sleeping peacefully after drinking a large bowl of milk and the birds were picking up the grains the boy's mother had scattered on the grass. The rat was eating a ripe mango that had appeared right under his nose but he was taking quick, nervous bites in case the mango turned into a slippery slipper again.

Then the boy came out and stood looking at the birds. He could not imagine why he had ever wanted to harm them. A tiny bird came and perched on his arm. He stood very still. The bird sang a few notes and flew away. He could not understand what the bird had said but it sounded a bit like 'Thank you'.

Bubo rubbed his hands with glee. Now what prank should he play next, he thought as he changed himself into a silvery meteor. His battery was fully charged again. He shot up into the sky.

100000035 feet in 15 seconds: A world high-jump record for spooks.

NOTES ON THE MISCHIEF-MAKERS

ADITHI RAO graduated from Smith College, USA, with a degree in Theatre, and returned to India to work as an assistant director on the award-winning Hindi film *Satya*. She has written *Shakuntala & Other Timeless Tales from Ancient India* and *Growing Up in Pandupur* (co-authored with her sister Chatura). Adithi also writes film scripts, the rights to one of which have been bought by Aamir Khan Productions Ltd. Over the years, her short stories for children have appeared in anthology collections published by Scholastic, Puffin, Wisdom Tree, HarperCollins and Young Zubaan.

ARUNAVA SINHA translates classic, modern and contemporary Bengali fiction, non-fiction and poetry into English. Forty of his translations have been published so far. Born and educated in Calcutta, he lives and writes in Delhi.

When BIJAL VACHHARAJANI is not reading Harry Potter, she can be found traipsing around the jungles of India. In her spare time, she works as a consultant editor and writes about education for sustainable development. Bijal has a Masters in Environment Security and Peace from the University of Peace in Costa Rica. She is the author of two children's book, *So You Want to Know about the Environment* and *What's Neema Eating Today?*

BULBUL SHARMA is a painter and writes for children and adults. Her books for children include *Tales of Fabled Beasts*, *Gods and Demons* and *The Ramayana for Children*. She conducts 'Storypainting' workshops for special needs children and is a founder-member of Sannidhi, a NGO that works in village schools.

GILLIAN WRIGHT is a translator and writer based in New Delhi. She has translated two classic novels of Hindi literature, *Raag Darbari* by Shrilal Shukla and *A Village Divided* by Rahi Masoom Reza, as well as a selection of the acclaimed short stories of Bhisham Sahni. Her other books include *Mishti, the Mirzapuri Labrador, Presidential Retreats of India* and *The Darjeeling Tea Book*. She has also worked with her partner Mark Tully on all of his books, co-authoring *India in Slow Motion*.

JERRY PINTO lives and works in Mumbai. He was not a mischievous child as he remembers his childhood but then no one remembers being mischievous.

It took KAVITHA MANDANA many years to figure out that when you're the tallest in class, you ALWAYS get caught for not just your own pranks but even those played by other, smaller, more invisible mischief-makers. She currently works full time with a technology firm editing journals. Her children's books have been published by Puffin, Red Turtle and Karadi Tales. She also writes and illustrates for *Deccan Herald*'s children's newspaper.

Khyrunnisa A. is a prize-winning author of children's fiction. She created the popular comic character Butterfingers for the children's magazine, *Tinkle*. She carried the character over to the hilarious Butterfingers series of books published by Puffin. She also writes regularly for the magazine *Dimdima* and has an ongoing fortnightly column, 'Inside View', in *The Hindu Metroplus*. She worked as Associate Professor of English at All Saints' College, Thiruvananthapuram and now spends her time twiddling her thumbs when she isn't reading or writing.

Paro Anand is a Bal Sahitya Puraskar winner. She has written books for children, young adults and adults. Her book *No Guns at my Son's Funeral* was on the International Board on Books for Young People Honour List. *The Little Bird Who Held the Sky up with His Feet* was on the list 1001 Books to Read Before You Grow Up, an international gold standard of the world's best books ever.

R.K. Narayan was born in Madras in 1906. Narayan wrote twelve novels, five collections of short stories, two travel books, two volumes of essays, a volume of memoirs, and re-told legends and epics. Narayan, who lived to be ninety-four, died in 2001.

Ranjit Lal is the author of over thirty-five books for children and adults who are children. His abiding interest in natural history, birds, animals and insects is reflected in many of his books. His book *Faces in the Water* was honoured by IBBY in 2012, won the Crossword Award for Children's Writing 2010 and the Ladli National Media Award for Gender Sensitivity 2012. *Our Nana Was a Nutcase* won the Crossword Raymond Award for Children's Writing in 2016. His other interests include photography, automobiles, reading and cooking. He lives in Delhi.

RUSKIN BOND has written novels, memoirs, short story collections and books of essays and poetry. He was awarded the Padma Shri by the Government of India in 1999 and the Padma Bhushan in 2014.

SHRUTHI RAO (http://www.shruthi-rao.com) is a writer and editor. *Manya Learns to Roar* is her latest book for children. She loves books, trees, desserts, and hikes. She gets pranked more than she pranks (much to her chagrin).

SUBHADRA SEN GUPTA has earned her grey hair writing for children and loves writing on history and scripting comic strips. The story you read here was written for a wonderful children's magazine called *Target* and much of what happens in the story is true.

SUKUMAR RAY was a poet, short story writer and playwright who wrote in Bengali mainly for children. His works such as the collection of nonsense poems *Abol Tabol*, novella *HaJaBaRaLa*, short story collection *Pagla Dashu* and play *Chalachittachanchari* are considered some of the finest writing for children in the world.

VANDANA BIST is a well-known Indian artist and writer celebrated for her exquisite use of detail and colour in her pen and ink drawings. She has won many national and international awards for her artwork. She has illustrated books like *Nine and a Half Fingers, The Princess with the Longest Hair, Panchatantra Tales, Awadhi Folk Tales* and *Surangini.* Her venture AkkaBakka takes art to children in exciting ways.

VINAYAK VARMA writes, designs and illustrates stories. Go say hi to him at www.mixtape.in

Ruskin Bond was born in Kasauli in 1934. He has written novels, memoirs, short story collections and books of essays and poetry. His books include the popular classics *Room on the Roof* (winner of the John Llewellyn Rhys Prize), *A Flight of Pigeons*, *The Blue Umbrella*, *Time Stops at Shamli*, *Night Train at Deoli*, *Our Trees Still Grow in Dehra* (winner of the Sahitya Akademi Award) and *Rain in the Mountains*. He was awarded the Padma Shri by the Government of India in 1999 and the Padma Bhushan in 2014.

Jerry Pinto is the author of the novels *Murder in Mahim* (2017) and *Em and the Big Hoom* (2012; winner of the Hindu Prize and the Crossword Book Award), and the non-fiction book *Helen: The Life and Times of an H-Bomb* (2006; winner of the National Award for the Best Book on Cinema). His children's books include *A Bear for Felicia*, *Monster Garden*, and *When Crows Are White*. In 2016, Jerry Pinto was awarded the Windham-Campbell Prize and the Sahitya Akademi Award.